Praise for:
Journey of Dreams
by Joan Bridgeman

"Throughout history, various cultures have endorsed the idea that a separate "astral body" disconnects from the physical body during sleep and is free to travel along the astral plane. Whether or not the reader agrees with the mystical content portrayed, the experiences described are quite interesting. This well-written, rather unusual book is commended to the open-minded reader. Dream interpretation can be a very revealing endeavor."

- S. M. King, M.B.A., M.Ed.

"*Journey of Dreams* is a diligent, comprehensive look by one who has recorded her dreams for over 40 years. Included is a fascinating look at what the author calls "odd dreams" . . . inclining this reader to think of anomalous phenomena. This book is an honest commentary on the vicissitudes of life. It is well-written and edited and the dreams are printed in bold in an easy-on-the-eyes font. This is some of the most valuable dream information I've come across.

Whatever your religious beliefs or lack thereof, *Journey of Dreams* offers much to contemplate. The author tells her story with sincerity and the belief that sharing this journey is her life's purpose."

- Maurice DesJardins

"Anyone who writes so openly about herself earns my complete admiration. Putting one's life into the public's eye is a courageous and bold action. *Journey of Dreams* is a beautiful human statement about how a family lives in this world. Her life's activity will survive in this book long after we are here to re-read it."

- A. J. O'Toole

SECRET CONTACT

Journey Beyond the Dreams

Joan Bridgeman

Azalea Art Press
Southern Pines, North Carolina

ISBN: 978-0-9899961-6-7

Dedication:

This book is dedicated to the memory of my parents who did their best to convince me that my vivid childhood dreams were just my imagination. I shut down all recall of dreams from the time I was four years old until I was thirty-one.

By then I was mature enough to handle my dreams. Forty-four years later I discovered that some of them were not just my imagination at all.

Mom always thought I was a "late bloomer" and she was right.

Other Books
by Joan Bridgeman:

Journey of Dreams—
40 Years of Dream Keeping
© 2011

CONTENTS

Preface

"Dreams are by far the most accurate
and secure way to gather intuitive information
that I've ever found."

- David Wilcock
http://DivineCosmos.com

These words may be unusual to you but you are already familiar with the *astral/etheric* and *spiritual planes, levels* or *dimensions* because you go to these places when you sleep. The experiences you have there are quite real. Sometimes the memories of your dreams can indicate what you were doing while your body was sleeping. The spiritual dimension is where you lived until you incarnated into a physical form. Now you visit there during sleep.

While you're sleeping it's normal to dream of people you once knew on Earth who have since passed on and now live full time in the spiritual world. Early in my remembrance of the dream state I was aware of nebulous forms around me. I never had any interest or interaction with them. The first person I recognized in a dream was my great-grandmother.

On July 31, 1973, I dreamed that she and I were at a concert seated side by side. Within the short dream I was surprised and delighted to see her again. Even now I remember her clear, brief image as she appeared in my dream—much younger and with dark hair. In some way she identified herself to me,

i

because when I knew "Grammy" on Earth she was a thin, elderly white-haired lady in her eighties.

February 1941
Jane O. Bridgeman (Mother), Amy H. Orchard
(Grandmother), Author Joan Bridgeman, Age 2,
Matie W. Orchard (Great Grandmother)

The last time I saw my great-grandmother in this reality was about 1950 when my family went to visit her and my grandparents. I was 12 years old then and Grammy was quite ill. My mother asked me to sit and visit with Grammy in the quiet alcove where she was propped up on a chaise longue. I remember that occasion vividly even now. Grammy did a lot of talking— but she wasn't speaking to me. She carried on a soft conversation with someone she called "Chas." He seemed to be suspended in the air above and slightly behind me. I sat there stunned; observing, listening and totally fascinated.

Later, on the drive home, I asked my mother,

"Who's Chas?" Mom spun around in the front passenger seat with a look of shock on her face. "Where did you hear that name?" she asked. I told her that Grammy had been talking with him for a long time and didn't seem to know I was even there. Mom told us that Chas was Grammy's husband who had died a long time ago.

I think that because I had known my great-grandmother, the fact that she was in my dream seemed perfectly normal—or at least okay—because I never questioned it!

Five years later, I had a very short dream where **"a man named Cyrus who had already died, is helping me get into the best classes."** The fact that he had *already died* was being impressed upon my mind simply by the way I recorded the dream. This was my first conscious realization that *all* those people in my dreams were actually spirits!

Introduction

"To thine own self be true."

"Hamlet"
- William Shakespeare
(1564-1616)

For 75 years now I've lived on this planet believing that I'm just like everyone else, more or less. The only deep, dark secret I had was that I nearly committed suicide when my first marriage was collapsing in 1969. I was 31 years old and my life was a wreck. At the last moment, I suddenly became totally immobilized and a disembodied voice boomed out, "**You cannot leave your children**!" Then, inside my right ear, a gentle voice spoke softly and repeated the same words. I understood then that I had heard The Truth.

After this supernatural event, I began to have exceptionally vivid dreams. They were almost more real than my waking life and I felt a strong compulsion to write them down. Morning after morning I filled a page or more with complex situations that I couldn't understand. However, I felt that these dreams were somehow important and continued to record them. Year after year the journals piled up, filled with hundreds of dreams that I never had the slightest interest in re-reading. At times very strange things seemed to be happening to me but I pushed these thoughts away and stayed grounded in my "real" life.

In 2009 I received a forwarded e-mail from an author in the United Kingdom. He was requesting dreams for a book he planned to write. I sent him 51 dreams and he responded, "Thank you! Your dreams are wonderful, so detailed and well written. Why don't you write your own book?" I had no idea how to do something like that and wasn't the least bit interested. When I awoke the next morning, the first thing in my mind was, "Oh yes, I could write a book; I *should* write a book about my dreams!"

And so it was that I began to re-read more than 2,000 dreams that had accumulated over the past 40 years and to pick out the most interesting ones. I decided to use my maiden name as author and titled the book *Journey of Dreams—40 Years of Dream Keeping.* My early life is chronicled in it.

Now I've been tasked to write a second book. This one reveals an incredible little secret, which slipped past me in that first book. *Journey of Dreams* contains what I called odd dreams; so many, in fact, that I put a group of them in a separate section at the back of the book. Several weeks after publication in May 2011, I sat down and began to read my actual published book objectively. When I came across the first few odd dreams I began to get an uncomfortable feeling about them. But again, I pushed it to the back of my mind and concentrated on giving talks about dreams, selling the book and keeping up with a very busy life.

In September of that year, my evening Guided Writing (which will be explained in Chapter Three) indicated that I would be writing another book and would have help when it was time. Then, in March of 2012, this Guidance asked me to re-read all of my old dreams again because there would be new developments and discoveries in my life. Two months later while browsing in a local used books store, I picked up an old paperback. The title was *UFO Abductions in Gulf Breeze.* Immediately I had conflicting thoughts: I felt I needed to read this book but I wasn't sure I wanted to. However, I bought and read it. Some of the author's descriptions of being taken from his bed were exactly the same as I had experienced! I began to buy more books about UFOs and ETs. The similarities between those authors' experiences and my dreams and feelings were astounding! Finally I had to face the realization that my odd dreams were truly memories of actual encounters with extraterrestrial aliens!

I have never consciously seen any of the short, large-eyed androids but I have felt the presence of something unnerving in my bedroom. Once I felt a strange hand take hold of my hand and pull me away, out of the room. While some authors describe very frightening experiences, others have a different perspective. Those were the kind of books toward which I found myself gravitating. Two of those authors kindly granted me permission to cite excerpts from their recent books.

In her book, *The UFO Agenda,* Diane Tessman says:

> *"I will not say that I was the victim of an abduction because that has never been my mindset or my experience. My experience was very strange but positive."*

Reverend Michael Carter, in his book, *Alien Scriptures*, states:

> *"I feel that my spiritual growth was somehow accelerated and that in spite of the emotional*

fear it engendered, this was a positive experience for me."

My current dreams and Guided Writings show that these encounters are ongoing and contain loving, enlightened Beings who, I believe are my Spiritual Guides. I have not consciously seen any of these Beings. They appear in my dreams as whitish vapor-like wisps or brightly colored lights.

Secret Contact begins where my first book ended and includes an entirely new selection of unusual dreams, experiences and Guided Writings. To be honest, it's uncomfortable to open my personal world to public scrutiny but I truly believe that I've been guided and led to do this. I must step out of my comfort zone. However, I also know that I'm just one of hundreds of thousands of people who came into the world with this kind of mission. Perhaps my coming forward now will encourage others to do the same. **I am a contactee. My mission is to share my truth.**

Long ago I was told that the shivers that sometimes run down the back of my neck are a signal from Spirit. They indicate that whatever I've just heard or said is Truth. This usually happens during one-on-one conversations and, if I say, "Oh, that just gave me goose bumps!" nearly always the other person admits to feeling the same sensation. When I first began reading about other authors' encounters with extraterrestrials, I often got these chills. Below is a list of the feelings and experiences of those writers, which match the feelings and experiences in my life and recorded dreams. When you read this long list of synchronicities, you may recognize some of them yourself, especially if they give *you* goose bumps!

CONTACT EXPERIENCE HIT LIST

Feelings/Emotions
Strong feeling of being watched
Feeling that you are 'different'
Body shaking, rocking or vibrating
Feeling emotionally isolated
Half-awake, paralyzed and knowing that someone or
    something is in the room
Feeling frightened and then falling asleep or being put
    to sleep
Feeling that you are being protected, watched over
Feeling that you're being guided and taught during your
sleep

Sound/Sight/Sensation
Hearing buzzing, whirring, humming, whirling sounds
Seeing owls in holograms, dreams, visualizations
Being pulled out of bed and taken (flown away)
Floating through walls, doors or other solid objects
Flying, gliding, floating, hovering in space
Feeling G-forces from rapid acceleration
Flying in a vehicle low to the ground
Moving or being held in a force you can't get out of
Being flown backwards
Riding along an escalator, conveyor belt or moving
    sidewalk

People/Other Beings
People are present but you can't see them
Seeing a person but not the face
People interact but stay behind you
Everyone communicates telepathically
Wispy, white forms float or fly past
Recognition of someone you don't see

Buildings/Structures
Huge structures like airports
Underground facilities, caverns
Buildings with white walls, long, wide hallways and
    many rooms

Hospital/Clinic Settings
Lying on examination table that molds itself to your
    body
Enormous rooms with hundreds of people lying on
    tables
Being examined by doctors and/or nurses

Places
Out in the universe
On another planet
Taken back or ahead in time (time traveling)
In another dimension
Aboard a craft, UFO, spaceship

Special Abilities, Attributes, Beliefs
Feel enlightened in some way
Notice many coincidences in life
Believe you've been prepared for some benevolent
    purpose

Been in touch with another realm of existence
Believe extraterrestrial aliens act as spiritual guides
Believe that extraterrestrials are benevolent Beings
Special information has been put into your mind
Believe that somehow you agreed to participate in this
    relationship
Believe you are in contact with a higher consciousness
Believe you can communicate telepathically
Believe your dreams are important
Have vivid and sometimes psychic dreams and
    visualizations

Many people all over the world are having contact experiences during their sleep. These are not "just dreams"—they are *real* events, remembered in the form of dreams. It's very possible that you, who have been drawn to read this book, may discover that you are a contactee too!

"Nature has planted in our minds
an insatiable longing to see the truth."

- Marcus Tillius Cicero
Roman Orator, Poet, Statesman
(106-43 B.C.)

CHAPTER ONE

Sleep, Dreams
& the Mind

SLEEP, DREAMS & THE MIND

Dreams are mental and emotional experiences that occur when your physical body sleeps. They are real events that take place in other dimensions. Everyone dreams four or five times during the night although most people don't usually recall more than one dream, if that.

Before you reach the dream world you first need to "fall asleep." Everyone knows that the physical body requires rest and sleep to stay healthy. However, there's a part of you that never sleeps. It's called the astral (astral means relating to the stars) or soul body. The Earth plane and our physical bodies are denser than the astral energy and the vibratory rate is much slower. The astral body is amorphous, vapor-like. It looks misty and has a faster vibratory rate than the physical body. When you go to sleep, your astral essence releases itself and slips out of your physical form. It remains connected to your physical body by the astral or "silver cord" through which all autonomic functions continue. This cord stretches as far as it needs to go and has a faint silvery glow, which resembles frost. It cannot disconnect accidentally. At the moment the astral form slips out of the physical body, there can be a slight twitch. If you're aware of this transition, a momentary paralysis may occur. This can be frightening but under normal circumstances your body will simply "let go" and your astral form will move away into the astral dimension. When it's time for you to wake up, your astral form unerringly follows its cord back to your sleeping physical body.

There are different types of dreams; some review events of the previous day. Others can help you solve

3

problems or perceive issues in your daily life more clearly. Amazing inventions and plots for successful novels have been created as a result of dreams. There are dreams that deliver messages and other interesting phenomena that can occur in a dreamlike state. These will be addressed in the forthcoming chapters. The most important dreams are the ones you remember. Many of my dreams arrive between two and four o'clock in the morning. If they're strong enough to wake me, I know they need to be written down. Any dream that wakes you is worth recording because it very likely contains information that another part of your mind wants to bring to your conscious attention. That information will usually prove to be helpful in your waking life.

There are different levels of the mind—the Con-scious mind is the part you use when you're awake. This is the level in use right now as you read this sentence. The Subconscious, also called the Unconscious mind, takes in and stores everything that happens in your life, whether you're aware of the events or not. For instance, there are sounds within your hearing at this moment but unless you stop reading to pay attention to your environment, you're not consciously aware of them. However, your subconscious is taking them in. During sleep, any of these subconscious memories may work their way into a dream. Parts of programs you watched on television, conversations you had or over-heard can turn up in your dreams during the night.

There is a third level of mind called the Super-conscious, a word which was coined by Edgar Cayce, "The Sleeping Prophet." Cayce described the superconscious as a higher realm of the subconscious; a place where universal forces can be contacted to provide information and guidance. Many of the dreams I record come from my superconscious mind.

Most people think that dreams don't make any sense; that they're impossible to understand. This assumption is partially correct because dreams often speak in a language called *symbolism*. A symbol is an image that represents something. For instance, a dream that takes place at a beach sounds like an enjoyable setting. A beach is a place where it appears as though the water and the earth meet. Symbolically, it's the place where the subconscious mind contacts the conscious mind. I love the beach with its feeling of open space, the view of endless ocean, warm sun and sand, fresh air and blue skies. However, if you don't care for beaches, this will affect your feeling and reaction to the scene. The symbols that your subconscious mind chooses to display in your dreams are specifically your own. I think the beach may represent the dream world to me, a place where I am comfortable. The *condition* of the beach (weather, wind, sun or lack of sunshine) adds further information and meaning to the dream. The brighter the light is in your dream, the more clearly you're able to see what is intended for you to perceive and understand and the more positive the dream may be. Dreams from the superconscious level are bright and usually accompanied by joyous feelings.

Here's a short dream I had on September 16, 1984. I didn't notate the times of my dreams in those early years but all of them were in the morning hours of the dates given.

There are crystals all over the beach! I'm pointing them out to the people around me who don't realize how special and precious they are. We gather them up to share with people who will appreciate them. These crystals are of many different sizes and shapes and all of them are gorgeous!

Crystals are noted for their healing properties as well as clarity of thought and they represent an elevated level of consciousness. Crystals are also recognized as power sources. The "people around me" are nebulous figures, most likely spiritual forms as well as the astral forms of humans whose physical bodies are sleeping at home.

7/28/79
In the midst of a long dream I turn the page in a songbook and see a paragraph in quotations. It's very meaningful to me. It begins, "The strength of life is in the Truth" and it continues for about 12 more lines. It's printed in black ink on a white page on the left side of the book.

This was all I remembered and recorded. A song book is not an unusual symbol in my dreams because I've been involved with music all my life. Symbolically, the left often represents the past and I believe this message concerns the past. Black and white infer clarity, something that can be easily understood in one way or the other. Turning a page indicates moving forward. This is what these symbols mean to me, the dreamer. Feelings are important to note and I remarked that the message was meaningful—it has a purpose which resonates within me. The short quotation is significant because it stood out so clearly and refers to what I believe is my mission in this life. The page on the left is my first book in whose pages I "sang my song" by sharing my life and 40 years of my unusual dream world. Without the flash of insight (perhaps a nudge from my Guidance) as I re-read that book after its publication, I would not have suddenly understood that the odd dreams were actual memories of very strange and real experiences. I understand this dream quite clearly now and it's time to muster my courage, come forward and tell my Truth.

More recently, I had a dream with a message which I believe is about this present book.

3/6/13 - 3:15 a.m.
I'm supposed to be going somewhere, doing something. There are two or three energies nearby encouraging me to be ready. I don't see them but I distinctly *feel* their presences. My mind is sluggish—confused and overwhelmed by many distractions. I *do* want to cooperate and begin to seriously attend to what they are urging me to do but I don't have much stamina right now.

This dream was elusive! It came and went as I lay there not able to wake up quite enough to write it down at 3:00 a.m. It was taking me a long time to recover from the flu I got in January. I had been told via Guided Writing on September 24, 2011 that I was to write another book. They were reminding me that time was passing. I was almost too tired to think.

Over the years I have recorded innumerable contacts with what I call my Spiritual Guidance. These are Teachers, Counselors, companions, friends and others whom I seldom see but whose familiar energy or "presence" I feel. Each living entity, whether embodied in flesh or discarnate, exudes an individual energy or vibration. Many humans, awake or asleep, have dreamed or felt the familiar 'presence' of a deceased loved one and known who it was even though the entity wasn't seen. What I have been allowed to see are glimpses of things like a sandal-clad foot, the hem of a white robe, shining, lustrous hair and bright flashes of colored lights. Often in dream situations I understand that these others cannot actually do anything for me. I'm the only one who can make a decision or cause something to happen. Their purpose seems to be mainly supportive.

Many of these Beings with whom I interact regularly in my dreams are loving and helpful Guides, Teachers and Counselors. They're not what most people currently think of when we hear the term "extraterrestrial aliens." Some of the other authors, who also have had positive experiences with these "Visitors," have found these Beings very willing to help humanity. I cannot yet speak from personal knowledge except for what my dreams show. However, I do recognize a type of Being who does take charge at times. This kind accompanies me to visit unusual places and also has the authority to tell me important things, most of which I don't recall when I wake. My mission is to help build a bridge between a struggling humanity and those who truly wish to help us.

The next section of this book presents all the odd dreams that were not published in *Journey of Dreams*. The Guided Writing section follows that and will be thoroughly explained with a wide sampling of the writings themselves. The remainder of the book contains a variety of dreams and experiences which may serve to amuse, surprise and perplex the reader.

"The unexamined life is not worth living."

- Socrates
(469 B.C. - 399 B.C.)

CHAPTER TWO

Contact

My dream life began toward the end of 1969. The dreams in this section begin in 1970 when the "odd" ones first started. During the early years of recording dreams I didn't add any commentary or indicate the times of the dreams. This collection of dreams, which are *memories* of the events and experiences you are about to read, are just as I recorded them on the dates given. No matter how strange they may have seemed at the time, I simply typed and filed them in notebooks without ever reading them until 2009. Now, in 2013, after reading other books on dreams, I'm able to add comments which explain and/or verify that these dream events are encounters in other dimensions.

ET & UFO DREAMS

8/28/70
There's a medical office in a place like a barn loft. The doctor comes into the room where I'm waiting. He's new to me and I think he's a temporary summer replacement for the regular physician. He's very pleasant and surprisingly interested in my feelings and opinions. I don't recall why I came here but I mention that I had a few stomach cramps. He reaches right into my stomach and abdomen with both hands and "adjusts" something. When I leave, I walk carefully down an outside stairway.

10/6/70
I'm lying on a hard table in an operating room that seems like a large factory. It's brightly lighted and very clean. The doctor stands or half-sits on a stool at my left and the nurse stands over me on my right.

Both doctor and nurse are dressed in crisp white. Evidently I need my nose fixed. The doctor insists that the nurse do the surgery and seems amused at her obvious discomfort. She holds a small transparent vial of tiny wooden slivers. I ask if she's going to drop them down into my nostrils and sinuses. She says no and, holding two of them with tweezers, lights a flame to them and places one at each nostril. I feel no pain but there's a bright flare-up of sparks which causes her to flinch back. The flames go out.

No wonder people think dreams are weird. And yet, when you have the opportunity to examine them many years later with a lot more knowledge and understanding, there's a sense that they have validity. I don't know whether I was given an implant but I've had sinus issues most of my life.

One experience I'll never forget is when I went to the infirmary during my freshman year in college. I had a horrible headache which turned out to be a sinus infection. The doctor wrapped cotton strips around long metal clips, soaked them in a pungent-smelling liquid and then pushed these far up into my nostrils. They were painful but I felt nearly terrified emotionally the entire time I had to wait until he finally removed them and let me leave. I have a suspicion now that this was related to a subconscious encounter experience.

12/18/70
Sleeping on an outside balcony or porch, I just *know* something is going to happen to me and I'm fearful and distressed. Then I see five men dressed alike in blue and black checkered hunting jackets coming

along the dimly lighted street below. They continue right on up the walls to where I am.

This apprehension is a typical hypersensitive reaction to the approach of the Greys prior to an abduction or contact. Apparently they can disguise themselves or cause a human to see something that isn't really there. They also can levitate and go through walls, doors and other solid three-dimensional objects.

7/17/71
A man appears at a party and comes over to where I'm sitting. He takes hold of one of my hands and professes to be reading my force field. Later, a girl tells me he was making lightning flashes fly from his fingertips.

This sounds like magic. However, I remember hearing the surprising crackling sounds of sparks flying off a young woman's hands when she was doing healing work in a class I attended in the late 1980's. Out of the ordinary things happen in this physical world, too!

6/12/73
In a small unfamiliar apartment, I'm lying on a couch feeling paralyzed as though overcome by a very strong force. I fight it, attempting to see what it is and eventually it releases me.

The transporters have a very strong psychic energy but apparently not the kind of physical strength to wrestle or fight off an upset human who is resisting with every ounce of determination she can muster.

"Releasing me" could also imply that I was simply put to sleep and only *thought* I'd won the fight! To this day, I have no recall of seeing one of these Greys except in other people's sketches and photographs.

6/26/78

Even though I'm sleeping, I am aware that at the far end of the room there's a pulsing bright mini-comet of greenish-white glowing light. At the front end I can occasionally perceive a cartoon figure which looks like a little lightning bug. I'm surprised but not frightened. Evidently I close my eyes and begin to feel a paralytic pressure–and then nothing more.

In the five years between this dream and the last, the transporters knew I was susceptible to the images they could project. Here I easily succumbed to their energies, released my astral form and went with them.

12/5/78

I'm part of a small group meeting air vehicles that are carrying people to our location. I run through long, empty corridors in search of the correct landing area so that we can escort these others to our location. Later, there's a scene of a crowded waiting room in a very old station; it's congested with strange characters who are only partly human. Our purpose or mission isn't clear, nor is it one that can be out in the open. However, we're a strongly united group, dedicated to the cause and very intent on carrying out the work we've agreed to do.

Apparently I knew my part in a secret mission, mingling with different humanoid races in another dimension. There were space shuttles or craft which I didn't recognize as planes. No descriptions of these humanoids were mentioned.

12/31/78
Lying in my childhood bedroom, I can feel myself rocking inside my body; then suddenly, I'm aware of a 'presence' hovering over me.

As soon as I completely released my astral form from my physical body, a Guide or transporter was there to escort me to the place of that night's work or assignment.

1/3/79
I rise, floating smoothly upward on an escalator into a large, bright building. I'm going to a meeting. Then it seems like a hospital or institution of some sort.

I think this was a typical out-of-body contact event. After being flown out of the bedroom, many contactees are taken into a UFO hovering nearby. There, they are examined, tested and healed from exposure to toxins and pollutants in the Earth's atmosphere. Most of the time their memories are wiped clear of anything they've experienced and possibly other images may be implanted.

1/16/79
In the midst of a long dream in which I am 12 years

old, a funeral director-like man explains either that "the room is very deep in the earth or very elevated." That's why we are experiencing a feeling of pressure, like a sudden attack of dizziness.

I have no recollection of this dream or what it could mean. I was out-of-body in an unusual environment that caused a strange sensation to my astral form. This may have been one of my first experiences of changing dimensions in a fast-moving spacecraft.

1/28/79

There's a rumbling sensation deep in the earth, a steady tremor. I'm floating in the upper part of a tall building, stretched out on my back about three-quarters of the way to the ceiling. I glance down to my left and see rows of tables on which other people lie looking up at me and around at each other. Then the room or building seems to tip a little, like a large ship rolling. I float feet first toward the far wall, as if caught in a slight pull of gravity. I don't know what occurred prior to this scene or why I'm lying stretched out like this but something is definitely wrong. Maybe this is a hospital and I'm being examined. It's not clear. However I'm very aware that this entire structure is moving somehow and I don't know what's going to happen.

Evidently I was on a large space craft experiencing a change in gravity. This was fairly early in my experience of having "odd dreams" and I had no idea what was happening or why.

18

4/10/79

A group of us have projected ourselves into another dimension in a spirit of fun. It's an experiment and an adventure to see what we can learn. There are two entirely different places where we go. The first has a tall, square stone tower with pink flowers covering its upper portion. It's a focal point in the main village square in a place like Sweden or Holland, perhaps. We're dressed in pink costumes and gowns. Whatever the occasion, it hasn't happened yet.

Then the scene shifts to gigantic waves on an ocean. We're in some sort of marine craft, being transported into this second dimension. At the end, (and there's missing time here) instead of being allowed to go back, we will somehow be 'wiped out.' When it's time to go where our "real reality" is, our consciousness will be gone, and we won't be able to say, "So long; I'll see you again sometime," or remember our experience here at all.

The first section of this speaks for itself; I was with others on an astral or spiritual plane. The color pink represents love, healing and well being. The second portion seems like a meeting with the ETs who are teaching and training us. They have the ability to wipe our minds clear so that our conscious daily lives are not impeded in any way by strange memories. "Missing time" is a real event in abduction scenarios. The gaps in dream sequences no doubt are the same . . . events that we're not allowed to remember are absent.

5/2/79

An energetic young man with brown hair comes bouncing through a doorway. I notice that he has a raised lump on the top of his head.

I've had a very quick look at someone! Many times, even now, I ask to see my Guides but never see anything except colored lights and extraneous bits. The entities who have evolved to the state of Light Beings are able to take on a physical appearance if they choose to. The lump on his this man's head is an interesting feature and apparently what I was to notice.

5/10/79

In a place like a college infirmary, I'm lying on a cot, half-conscious. Beside me is a container like an iron lung machine with glass sides. Now, more alert, I see a dead man lying in it and I understand that there's something significant about one of his hands. I'm very aware of this particular hand of the body lying here beside me. I get up slowly, either hesitantly or with difficulty walking, and go to another room. A nurse and two other people are here. They're surprised to see me up and tell me I must go back to my bed.

College indicates a teaching/learning situation and the infirmary infers a medical procedure or illness. The significance of the corpse's hand has no meaning to me. If I saw that hand clearly, the memory was wiped from my mind. Understanding the significance of that hand indicates that mental telepathy was used to point it out to me.

20

6/6/79

I'm adventuring with a small group of people in a strange place. Suddenly there is shuddering and shaking of the ground, like an earthquake. Things are beginning to break up all around us. Then, I'm walking very carefully inside a hollow cylindrical tube with slatted sides. The light, which is coming in from outside, has an orangey cast to it. The atmosphere is quite unusual and I'm afraid that these slats might close up. I'd prefer to be outside this cylinder if that happens and I begin to move carefully toward the side to find a way out. Immediately, I'm aware that something has just shifted and is now beginning to revolve in the opposite direction.

This entire experience was unusual and frightening. I don't think I was on the Earth during this dream.

8/19/79

I'm a passenger in a car being driven by a former childhood friend who moved away when we were both about seven years old. Behind us, an odd white object is coming down from the sky. It looks like some sort of rocket with gray smoke coming from its lower 'legs' and moving rather fast. I think it might crash—and sure enough, a few minutes later there is a ground-shuddering thud. Billows of black smoke and tendrils of flame shoot up beyond the shrubbery and trees in the distance. Almost immediately it rises again, hovers in the air, rotates and lifts up. It seems rocket-propelled yet also capable of hovering like a helicopter. Suddenly it takes off at a 45° angle at high speed. A moment later we hear a blast of sound

which startles us until we realize it must be the now-vanished flying vehicle.

Something may have occurred when this friend and I were seven years old, playing in the back field or riding bicycles around the neighborhood. The description certainly fits a space craft.

8/27/79

Apparently I'm one of the new recruits in a military organization of some sort. My assignment is to work in a large ship or submarine. We have to swim through many turning corridors or tunnels.

There are UFOs that dive and submerge underwater. In our astral forms we humans are able to glide and fly in any element, including the ocean because we're unencumbered by lungs and noses.

9/13/79

There are special meetings which are held a long distance away and occasionally I make an attempt to get there. This one has caught me by surprise because two men from the army are here. They're very pleasant and polite. One comments on my apparel and I notice I'm wearing a large piece of cotton cloth draped around me, held by a cord at my waist. It's makeshift but is the kind of robe I wear to the meetings. The men show me two packages of important photographs. They're grayish-black and white, rather unusual in some way and depict groups of people at an event. The men tell me the significance of these people (but this information isn't recalled

when I wake). Then they remind me that I'm to go to the special meeting and that they've come to escort me there.

This dream showed that I no longer needed to be taken from my bed by any entity, but required assistance getting to these meetings. I knew how to get where I needed to go, although the phrase, "I attempt to get there," indicated that it wasn't a simple process! I didn't record what color cloth was draped around me but find it interesting that the garment was brought to my attention. My memory was wiped clear of whatever the photographs showed.

12/13/79
I ride up in the elevator of an unfamiliar building and climb onto a shelf where I find children's clothing. I try on an unusual one-piece suit which has built-in feet! It appears quite small yet it stretches out as I pull it on gently. It glistens like a soap bubble, as though wet or rubbery. It covers my entire body and feels very comfortable.

From what I've read, the Greys, which are androids, wear tight-fitting one-piece suits. I don't know if their suits are shiny but this short dream is quite descriptive albeit rather strange. Why would I try on one of these little suits? The initial scene indicates moving upward, possibly into a UFO.

1/16/84
Three other people and I are seated in the back of a small, open aircraft, which is flying so low that it's

just barely over the street. It's moving smoothly and quickly. It's not on wheels, but not really in the air either. How strange.

This was all I wrote about this 30-year-old dream. It could have been my impression of 'group travel' where there is no vehicle at all. I may have been held in a strong energy field by three Greys, all of us in astral form.

3/17/84

In a hospital-like place, I'm lying on a table, feeling nervous because I'm about to have an operation. Another woman is on a table nearby. Her surgery isn't completed because the doctor hasn't gotten out whatever he needs. While I lie here waiting, a large gray seal on a low gurney is put beside me. The seal is lying on its back and has the vague shape of a woman. I mention this and someone confirms it. Then the seal rolls over and moves to my left hand, which is dangling over the side of my table. I feel the seal licking my hand. The female doctor is doing something to the back of my head or neck while I'm distracted by the seal. It seems she will remove something from me but it's not a serious operation. I trust these people and am not afraid.

What would this doctor be removing from the back of my head or neck? What's happening to the other woman? What's with the seal?

7/4/89

I'm in someone's kitchen asking a man about my

24

own age to stay for a meeting or class of mine, which will take place later this evening. The man gently puts his hands on my shoulders, looks into my eyes and says, "You don't realize how far away my home is." He's dressed all in white, in something that gives the impression of flowing sheets and I realize we must be at a costume party. We talk a moment about the distance from here to where he lives and then he agrees to stay to make a brief appearance and a short address to my class. I'm delighted and hurry away to get ready. I decide to wear my nun's costume, which is also all white.

This comment is rather humorous and naïve 25 years later, but who wore flowing robes except clergy and people at parties? It's curious that I would think I had a white nun's habit. There may be orders of nuns who wear white but I've been a Protestant all my life. Symbolically, white indicates spirituality and purity. One of my Spiritual Guides did take form in this dream but even though he looked into my eyes, I didn't recall seeing his face.

There's a gap here of twenty years. During this time I had ten odd dreams, which were published in my first book. In my personal life during this interim, I was active in community and dinner theater productions and sang in a ladies' barbershop quartet, which performed regularly in the area. My father passed on in 2000. I bought a new computer in January 2001 before I retired in June, and remarried in October 2001. The computer crashed in 2007, taking with it two full years' worth of dreams.

6/10/10

On a large ship somewhere, I'm feeling somewhat "captured" as though being held or kept here. I'm not frightened in any way; I simply don't have a sense of freedom. This ship is either at anchor or just meandering somewhere, purposely staying away from the land, which isn't a safe place right now. My feeling is that something has happened on or to the land and this deep ocean environment is more stable. I also sense that there are a lot of people here; we're all being kept safe. This huge cruise ship is being used as a rescue or "salvation craft". I'm seques-tered in my own room at this moment but am not be-ing held or kept prisoner.

This was a quasi-dream/visionary scenario. It's as though a small aspect of my future was placed under a microscope for a few seconds. I felt no emotion. This ship also could be a huge space craft moving smoothly in the atmosphere high above the earth.

8/14/10 - 2:00 a.m.

I'm acting as a liaison and reporter. A new type of extraterrestrial has arrived. I'm taking notes and discussing him with someone for a small group I work with. His outstanding feature is exceptionally large feet! He's lying on his back as I look at him and may be asleep, yet he's fully aware that he's under discussion. Evidently Earth, or wherever I am, has gone through radical changes. There are already several other types of ETs here living peacefully among us. This particular new one will be accepted; however, an introduction to society by way of media

26

or telepathic announcement will ease the transition. This will open the way for his acceptance and reduce surprise or any fearfulness when he appears among us. This extraterrestrial has other different and unique features but his feet are the most obvious.

I'm part of a team that coordinates new arrivals into this society. The ETs are very interested in helping Earth become a positive environment again. It's an important planet and is recovering from near-devastation. There are already five or six species of extraterrestrials here among us now and we all live peacefully together. However, each new arrival needs to be understood and introduced into the new society. It's an important job. Transition is vital for everyone here.

This job description is literally a "go-between" which is how my personal mission has been described. There is a definite sense of precognition in this detailed dream. I feel that these events will not occur within my present lifetime. (As I write these comments in late 2013, I am seventy-five years old and expect that I may have twelve or so years left on this planet.) However, I hope that these events *do* come into reality someday and, that there will finally be peace on Earth!

10/30/10 - 3:00 a.m.
I wake and glance at the clock but cannot rouse myself to write the dream. At 5:15 I wake and recall this:
There is a place where I go routinely during sleep. It's a long distance away and I'm escorted at super-

**speed astral travel far out of this world. It's a sched-
uled trip, part of a plan or duty that I have.**

No other memory or recall comes back except
this specific understanding.

11/2/10 - 5:00 a.m.
**Riding on a rapidly moving vehicle, I'm looking
through huge, very clear windows, seeing a terrain
of cliffs, canyons and rocky hills. The dirt and rock
cliffs are of various colors and textures—different
shades of browns, grays, reds and a yellowy mix of
hues at times. I've seen some of this area before. The
roadway we're traveling appears to be a crevice cut
into the cliffs. All the while, as we speed along, I talk
with a few other people who are very open and
friendly. They don't actually speak—we converse in
telepathic conversation. I'm quite animated and feel
almost hyperactive in this vehicle. Whether we have
already experienced something exciting, or we're
about to do so when we get wherever we're going,
isn't clear. It's a bright, sunny day and we're literally *flying* at high speed through these canyons!**

If we are not in a UFO with large clear windows,
perhaps we are in "group travel" mode where we're
held together by a strong energy force moving us all as
one unit and no vehicle.

3/6/11 - 5:00 a.m.
**There's a small car with a square-shaped front and
no windows or top. It has stopped in front of where
I'm standing and is facing toward my left. Two**

people are in this vehicle and they look strange to me; they're quite small and are nearly caricatures of humans. The driver has almost no hair at all—just stringy wisps as though it had been burned or singed off. The passenger looks the same. I try to explain to the driver that they shouldn't or can't do what they intend, whether it's to go where they're headed or to take something they want.

I don't know if I'm in this country after a traumatic event or somewhere else that's totally unfamiliar to me. I'm standing outdoors on what may have been a roadway. There is rubble and debris all around; there are no buildings, vegetation or any signs of life here. I'm feeling tense, empty and 'different.' It's like an alien, foreign outpost, perhaps in some war-torn country or possibly on another planet.

Nothing in this entire situation was clear to me. It was not a pleasant experience and I woke with an uncomfortable feeling. The small humanoids were very odd and I think that I probably wasn't on planet Earth.

4/25/11
The scene is a very congested place where many family groups are clustered. It's a huge indoor pavilion-like building where different ethnic and cultural groups are gathered. This seems like an enormous airport which is being used as a temporary shelter for humanity. I know that we may be here for an extended time. I understand this is necessary but I don't comprehend any more than that. For everyone's sake, it must be this way. We all seem to be

29

gypsies here now.

This building has high ceilings and a sense of vastness that feels like it has the capacity to accommodate thousands of people. There seems to be a tacit understanding that only decent, compatible human beings have been allowed here. I have no sense of danger or worry as I literally wade through a group of little children. I know that I'm not trespassing or invading these other people's spaces. This is simply the way it has to be for now. We're being protected and taken care of and we are all willing to cooperate and make the best of the situation.

Prior to this scene, life was in chaos and confusion. There are familiar people around me here, so I know this is my area—however, things are not normal by any means.

As I drifted away from speaking with a pleasant semi-foreign man, I began wake from this dream. This is another dream memory I believe could be precognitive for a UFO rescue mission, saving some of humanity from a catastrophic disaster on Earth.

10/8/11 - 4:00 a.m.
I have a fleeting impression of someone close beside me on my right, helping me step down and off what seems like a train step or platform. There is a vehicle right behind us. I need support at this time and feel grateful for it. I don't see this person but know he is very strong. His arm may be around me or his energy overlapping mine just for a moment.

30

Evidently, I was just back from being in a space-craft and my Unseen Companion was supporting me momentarily for some reason. In the astral world, everyone is in astral form and can feel touch. I may have been a bit dizzy with the faster vibration of my astral form in the process of slowing down prior to returning to my physical body.

10/23/11 - 3:30 a.m.
I distinctly hear three clear tones in the right side of my head. The pitches are 3-2-3 in the musical scale, or mi-re-mi. It's not quite a bell-like quality but very gentle in tone. They are soft, distinct and purposeful and located about an inch higher than my ear but inside my head. Immediately I understand that this is a signal. I'm being alerted to the fact that I am somehow 'hooked in or connected.'

I had wakened at 3:30 with a dream and was mulling it over when I heard these chime-like sounds. Now at 5:10 a.m. as I sit up to record this event, whatever dream I had is long gone but I'm positive that I have received a signal.

I sent this experience to Diane Tessman, who responded:

> "I agree! Your 'tones' are exactly like how our friends know you are awake and, as you say, connected. *Close Encounters of the Third Kind* made a lot out of tonal notes, partly because it was based on actual experiences with the higher realms, the good UFO-nauts."

That evening my Guided Writing added a few comments:

We are here. Yes, your special Guide did indeed send you a signal; a message that he is near. You converse in your sleep and now, awake, you have heard three tones.

3/16/12 - 4:30 a.m.
In a hospital somewhere, an elderly, short-statured man walks toward me from the left. He has strikingly thick, white curly hair. Someone introduces us and we shake hands. I notice that his face has a slightly different shape than I'm used to seeing and his skin color is a ruddy reddish-orange and quite deeply lined. I have the impression that he's wearing a nice yellow jacket, shirt or robe.

This description wasn't too unusual except for the facial shape and skin color. The sketch I made after recording the dream shows the man's chin very pointed in a triangular-shaped face. Yellow indicates intelligence and optimism. If this man was wearing a robe he was surely a spiritual Being. I have other dreams recorded where the extraterrestrials had orangey-colored skin.

3/27/12 - 3:30 a.m.
I'm intently focused on a map or chart, mentally involved in some way in a very important plan to bring a group of individuals together. Each person will need to be picked up and quickly brought to a higher

area or level. It will be a tricky and dangerous maneuver to coordinate and time is short.

I'm observing this through someone else, sensing his tension and urgency although I'm not understanding the reason for it. The chart and this male Being is to my left and slightly below me. I'm hovering, suspended and possibly held here by this Being's strong energy which exudes extreme intellectual power and controlled focus at this particular moment.

On the map or chart, which looks like dark oilcloth or canvas, the individuals of concern appear as bright glistening beads of water. I have a sense of awe that I'm here in this place and able to feel the energy of this unusual Being, whom I never actually *see,* but who is most definitely present.

I'm thankful that my young female cat woke me at that moment or I never would have been able to remember this experience. I believe I was riding in a UFO with my Star Guardian.

The Guided Writing the next evening remarked:

Your dream experience was indeed an actual fact; you were brought by your Guardian to his ship and allowed to observe and share his thoughts for a few moments. You understood this upon recording it. When you wrote it down it had just occurred. You slept and were borrowed.

4/25/12

**Somewhere far away 'out there' I'm in the close
company of a very strong male presence. He's powerful in energy, focus and command. Whatever our
purpose and work, it is extremely important and requires my total attention and cooperation, which is
unquestioned. There is a rapid form of transporta-
tion involved in the way we hurtle through space together.**

As I recorded this event, I recognized the type of
travel from previous dreams. There's a specific dream
which I had on *April 26,* 2010—almost exactly two
years ago and previously published—where I compared
this strong male to a magnet and myself to an iron fil-
ing. I referred that dream and my comment to Diane
Tessman, who confirmed that this entity *was* my Star
Guardian! This was an awesome, very real experience
which I recalled consciously as a dream.

5/12/12 - 5:00 a.m.

**I'm in a very strange place. Two people, familiar Be-
ings, are with me. They stay out of sight and are not
able to interfere but may converse with me telepathically. There's a great deal of confusion here. I'm one
of many people who have been brought to this place
for safekeeping. We must stay here for a while; it
won't be permanent but that's all we've been told.
I'm on a bus-like vehicle that will transport us back
to our crowded quarters.**

**Now, in a congested area of the enormous building
where we are staying, I overhear a bit of conversa-**

34

tion among three people nearby. Apparently meetings have been started for people from the same areas where we used to live. A thought occurs to me, or
is telepathically placed into my mind by one of my
Guides, that it would be good for me to attend a
group. They meet on Sunday afternoons. I'll go to
these meetings now, but I will have a conflict when
the NFL season starts. I don't want to miss any of
my team's games. That thought immediately wakes
me.

This dream was similar to previous dreams and
others already published. They all clearly indicated that
a space craft will lift humans from the planet if necessary to save their lives. Despite the inconvenience of the
crowded quarters, my feeling was that we were in good
hands. I was being watched over by my Guides. The
surprising conscious awareness of my fondness for the
Carolina Panthers pulled me right out of this dream!

5/16/12 - 4:00 a.m.
In an unfamiliar place and somewhat disoriented,
I sense that I've been sick or under anesthesia and
haven't regained my bearings yet. There's a lot of
activity going on around me—forms or energies
moving about, yet it's very quiet here. Someone
brings me a cup or small bowl of liquid to drink.
At first I think it's tea because this kind, unseen
person asks me if I would like something added to
my cup. All conversation is telepathic. I ask for
sugar and am told that sugar isn't nutritious and is
not available here. Now I understand that this isn't
tea; it's a nourishing nutrient that I need. Also, I

understand that there are many other people like me who have been rescued and saved. We're being helped now to adjust to this new environment. I feel that I am out-of-body and somewhat "displaced"—but that I'm not dreaming.

Not only was this very clear dream another possible rescue by a UFO, it could also be precognitive. It's one of several similar scenarios. I'm including them all.

6/4/12 - 5:00 a.m.
I have a pleasant memory image of standing in the glass-enclosed cabin of a ship as it glides smoothly over the ocean. Beside me, to my left, is the captain of this vessel, someone I know and like. I'm watching the waves roll up and away from the starboard side as the craft cuts through the water. From where I'm observing, this vessel is about the size of a small cruise ship that could hold about 400 passengers. There's no land in sight nor is there any conversation at this moment when I "tune in" to the scene. I have no image of the male Being who is standing beside me; however, we know each other and he has been explaining things to me telepathically.

This craft was on the ocean but I understood that it also had the ability to lift up into the air and fly extremely high. This might be something I was told or had experienced before. I believe this figure is my Star Guardian.

8/7/12 - 5:30 a.m.

This is a very strange place, mountainous and wild. My parents and other family members are here with me, visiting, exploring or vacationing. We walk through an interesting wooded area and come to a waterfall with a deep pool at the bottom. We climb down to look at the pool but then find it nearly impossible to get back up the steep incline.

Our plight is noticed by others who are native to this land or planet. They're rather odd-looking beings who have come to our rescue. They indicate a place where we can climb back up. When I get there, I see what looks like a row of leather-covered lawn chair backs embedded into the ground with about four inches protruding from the surface. It's enough for a toe-hold and we're able to get back up again.

My father had most of the interaction with these unusual inhabitants. There is no doubt in my mind that they were an unknown race of humanoids and that we were aliens in their land—wherever it is. No other details were recalled.

7/21/13 - 4:30 a.m.

I'm working with a male I know from somewhere before this time. Our work is very important. There are others here too and we're all aware of the need to stay undercover and out of the public eye. There's a group or faction that will try to stop us from our goal.

Toward the end of the dream the other helpers have

left and the man and I are finishing up. He goes into the next room of this hotel-like place—a tall building with large glass windows—and attempts to call me on a radio-like appliance. It works for a moment when I adjust it to the correct frequency or channel; then it becomes jammed or scrambled. This isn't good because we need to be able to contact each other. We can't have our meetings anymore and this transmitter will be our lifeline. (As I'm recording this dream I have the feeling that a temporary season is over and we all need to separate and be on our own except for this vital method of communication.)

My friend/leader/co-worker hurries back into this room to fix my appliance. Suddenly, there's a multi-colored helicopter hovering outside the window. It's mostly bright yellow with a smattering of markings in blue, green and red-orange. There are two men in it, wearing large headsets and goggles. They've discovered us. This is a dangerous situation . . . and the dream ends!

If this male is my Star Guardian or one of my Spiritual Guides, we can communicate telepathically. If this is a true situation and the dream is precognitive, then the radio-like appliance may be a walkie-talkie or cell phone of some sort and, I have not yet met this man in real life. I'm not aware of bright yellow helicopters anywhere in this country but, according to the internet, in the U.K. and Canada yellow helicopters are predominantly search and rescue vehicles and sometimes for medical use.

10/15/13 - 4:00 a.m.

In an unfamiliar sandy area, I'm a passenger in a small open jeep with no top. A husband-like man is driving. There are sand dunes and an ocean vista everywhere I look. The sand is medium-tan colored, coarse and grainy. It's a bright, beautiful day. We come to a place where the vehicles are in a long line. It may be a crowded bridge or that people must wait for the tide to go out more before they can cross the water.

My companion says that he knows another way and turns to the right. He drives rapidly along the sand for a distance and then straight up a very tall dune. When we reach the crest of this dune the height overwhelms me. I ask him to stop for a minute because I'm a bit dizzy and my heart feels like it's spinning or expanding. (It's somewhat like the feeling I've had on a roller coaster just before that initial drop when everyone screams!)

The view here is only tops of sand dunes and distant ocean water. I can't see anything at all below us where the jeep is preparing to go.

Now there's a breath-taking plunge down the dune. Finally, I see a good-sized ocean pool at the base and the jeep splashes into and through it. We rapidly continue on across the sand, up and down smaller dunes and eventually come to a beach area. There are a lot of people here enjoying their vacations. These folks are a bit different-looking . . . and their energies feel different too. They interact animatedly with each other but I can't understand their language. The younger people stare back at me. They seem to be in their late teens to mid-twenties; their hair is almost white, short and slightly wavy as it stands up on the tops of their heads. Their bright blue protruding eyes look like glass marbles that are too large for their eye sockets!

My companion and I walk along the beach until we get to some buildings. Then he goes ahead of me and up a flight of stairs. I wait for him, trying to read the lettering on the upper glass part of this door but it's not in any form or language that makes any sense to me and the dream ends.

The setting, a beach, is symbolic of the place where the conscious and unconscious meet. This husband-like man is the Guide who has been with me my entire human life. The brightness of the dream indicates that we're in a spiritual dimension. Our vehicle, if indeed there even is one, maneuvers in impossible feats. My astral form may be attached to the strong energy field of my Guardian, which feels like being in a vehicle. When I was almost unconscious at the top of the highest dune, I believe my Guide may have gone, in that dimension, to the limit that a human astral form can handle. Then comes a joyride to the vacation spot of another race of humans with remarkable eyes. My Guide goes on to a higher level and I realize for certain that I'm in an alien place and wake up.

My life and outlook have changed considerably since 2009 when I discovered that I was to write a book about my dreams. However, that wasn't the end of my assignment; nor is this second book the end. The culmination of my mission will be a third and final book documenting the results of a series of hypnotic regressions. Whatever mysteries and information lie within my subconscious mind and are revealed during these regressions will be published in the last book of this trilogy.

There is yet another interesting aspect of the abduction/contact experience which has been a running theme in my dream life for many years. Again, some of this genre of dreams were previously published but quite a few more surfaced when I re-read all my old journals searching specifically for them. See the next page for the fascinating topic of pregnancies and babies!

PREGNANCIES AND BABIES

In the books that other contactees have written, there are details of their experiences of being used as egg and sperm donors for the propagation of hybrids or other babies.

Although I have no personal *conscious* knowledge of this interesting aspect of the abduction/ encounters, I do have a number of dreams which tell of pregnancies and babies unrelated to my waking life. In one of these previously published dreams, I saw and played with two daughters who were normal, human-looking children.

Fourteen of these unpublished dreams were discovered when I re-read my old journals. Until I can uncover subconscious memories regarding my personal experiences with these pregnancies and babies, I'm simply including these dreams as I recorded them at the time.

11/4/70
I'm pregnant and surprised about it. There are two doctors here, standing across the white-draped table from each other. One is blond and familiar to me. I don't recognize the dark-haired doctor. A nurse is standing nearby and comments that I must have been thrilled when they carried my baby through the halls the last time I was here. I don't seem to remember that.

6/18/71
A woman of my age is standing outside. She's quite pregnant. We discuss when we are each going to

have our babies. I'm very surprised later to realize that I'm not pregnant after all. (At the time of this dream I was 33 years old.)

8/23/71
I'm pregnant again and very upset about it!

In June of 1976, I had a total hysterectomy. Apparently that had no bearing on my dream life, for I continued to have dreams of being pregnant!

12/3/78
An unusual sort of aircraft has landed and I'm joined by someone very special. I have to take with me a small round ghost. When the sunlight gets behind it, I can see that it's a baby. Part of the left side of its head is caved in a bit but there are wispy blue outlines of its features. I take the little "ball ghost" because it belongs with me at this particular time in my life.

7/5/79
I'm upstairs in a bedroom somewhere. I think I might be pregnant and can't believe it. There's absolutely no possible way I could be and this is quite embarrassing. This just couldn't have happened. This entire situation has an ethereal and almost spiritual atmosphere about it. Eventually everything turns out all right somehow.

7/27/79
There's a woman nursing a naked baby. The child is exceptionally alert and the mother is very pleased

with this baby. We seem to be on a houseboat or something that's moving. I feel as though I live here. Someone comes by and says, "You don't have to do this anymore." I reply, "I know I don't have to—but I want to."

8/6/79
In a small and cramped space I'm trying to give my little baby a bath in a tiny kitchen sink. The baby is withdrawn and listless. He's conscious but his 'essence' is just not in him. He lets me do whatever I need to do. I understand that when he feels more comfortable, he'll return and be more responsive. I get him washed, put him in diapers and clean clothes and then carry him somewhere else.

10/17/79
There's a baby I'm caring for which could be mine—except I don't know where I got it! I climb into a bed with the baby to get it to go to sleep. I'm tired too and need some rest. After a short time I feel discomfort under the right side of my ribs and I find that the baby's foot has gotten under me. I move it carefully so as not to disturb the child.

2/25/84
I'm with a friendly compatible male caring for two babies, a boy and a girl who are less than five months old. They seem to be older because they can toddle around and are more alert than five-month-old babies usually are.

1/7/85

I'm lying in a single bed with white head-and foot-boards, tired but restless. Just as I finally relax, an oppressive "gripping' sensation comes over me and a male voice speaks inside (or very close to) my right ear. This startles me and I bolt awake again and notice that now there's a baby in the bed with me; a sweet-faced blond infant of about six months old. He somewhat resembles my son, Greg. I discover that he can talk! He's intelligent and compassionate and we lie there, having a nice conversation.

9/12/89

I'm led to a room by someone I don't see and a man whispers, "Surprise!" A small baby is asleep on the bed there. In my excitement at seeing it, I inadvertently wake the child. It whimpers a little and I notice the irises of its eyes are pale tan and very unusual. The baby's skin has a smattering of slightly raised growths or skin tabs but my attention is almost entirely focused on its strange eyes.

8/24/90

At a conference somewhere in a large group of people, I begin to go into labor. I'm placed on a table and, although there's no pain or discomfort, a doctor comes over and gives me a dose of sodium pentothal. Immediately I feel relaxed. I ask if I can watch the birth but there's no mirror here; only a yellow painted wall.

The doctor says, "It's a girl!" Instantly, in my mind's eye, I envision the baby's face as a living photograph. She looks exactly like baby snapshots of me. The doctor, whom I never *see*, places the baby on my solar plexus as he keeps up a steady flow of friendly chatter. I feel no discomfort; only joy and elation.

7/29/08 - 2:00 a.m.
I'm in an unfamiliar place in comfortable surroundings although I can't recall anything about it. I'm aware that a group of children has been discovered who had been long-stored embryos or genetically bred and were raised together. The details about their origins are fascinating and very unusual. The children all have slight builds, are somewhat Asian in appearance and very open and talkative. There's an easy-going, comfortable feeling throughout the dream.

5/13/10
I have a new infant—it's a *boy*! The setting is unfamiliar and seems quite transitory. I'm totally unprepared for this new arrival! There's a husband-like figure nearby and, although I don't actually see him, we converse easily. He's very nice but unable to do anything to help me. There are other people around too but they're quite vague and are only observing.

I don't recall giving birth to this infant—he's definitely a surprise! As I take a closer look at him, I see a similarity to my son Greg as an infant. There's no doubt in my mind—this *is* my child! He doesn't talk (like some unusual babies I've had in dreams) but his eyes are open and he's been looking around at his new surroundings. Suddenly he shows incredible strength and the ability to move quickly. Somehow he gets down to the floor and begins to crawl around the room! It's amazing to watch this infant behaving as though he's eight months old!

There may be a new and different idea or ability—a "child of the mind"—that will suddenly and unexpectedly come into my life. That was my perception in May of 2010. Now in December 2013, as I type the dream for this new book, I know what it represents! I think this 'child of the mind' is the surprise discovery that the odd dreams in my previous book are actually memories of events that occurred during my sleep! Two and a half years later, the Guided Writing had an interesting comment:

> *11/12/13*
> *Your last dream in* Journey of Dreams *found you pregnant. Yes, it took a while for you to find the humor in your dream . . . pregnant with another* book! *We have great humor and are pleased to bring a smile to your face.*

"The Mind unlearns with difficulty
what it has long learned."

- Lucius Annaeus Seneca, the Younger
Roman Statesman
(c.4 B.C. - 65 A.D.)

CHAPTER THREE

Guided Writing

What I call my "Guided Writing" began in June of 1978 and is explained in detail in my first book. Here's a recap: I attended my first meeting of a consciousness-raising group in a nearby town on Cape Cod, MA. That evening the guest speaker was a metaphysics teacher from the Boston area. The subject of her talk was Automatic Writing—the process of holding a pencil loosely in your hand over a blank sheet of paper, relaxing and allowing "an energy" to move that hand and write. There was no way I wanted to allow that! She talked us through a trial exercise. I went along with it and was glad that nothing moved my hand. We were encouraged to practice at home and share our experiences at the following month's meeting.

I liked the people in this group and wanted to continue going to their meetings, so I made a couple of half-hearted attempts to practice this writing during the next several weeks. On the third try the pencil in my hand wobbled! I stared at it incredulously as it slowly began to move and form a letter. Instantly I thought I knew what the entire word was going to be and, sure enough, that word eventually appeared. Then another letter started to form and again I knew what the word would be—so I pushed the pencil myself. If *I* could be the energy moving the pencil, I *could* do this. Even if it seemed that I was imagining the words or thoughts in my head, I was willing to write them down myself.

I realized that this wasn't what the teacher called Automatic Writing so I decided to call it *Guided* Writing. I wrote nearly every day from July of 1978 until mid-September 1979 when my life was changed suddenly and moved me from Massachusetts to North Carolina. Excerpts from those two years were published in

Journey of Dreams.

    I did no further writing until 1987. I discovered the notebook in 2009 while searching for old dream journals for my first book. The notebook had Guided Writings from June 28, the eve of my 49th birthday, until November 2, 1988. The following is a paragraph from September 27, 1987:

> *You have never before experienced such helplessness as a collective humanity. You will survive and continue on in depleted circumstances learning to work and pull together for the common good. No more selfishness, for to be independent will mean one does not survive. Cooperative effort will be the only means of survival. Loss of many treasured possessions, yes. Your soul is your most treasured element and it will be your main support.*

    Then another notebook turned up with a Guided Writing from March 10, 1989. I sent it to my friend "Raum" for confirmation that the information *could* be from a source beyond myself. The following is excerpted from the longer writing:

> *We are here. We need you to continue writing; you are being fine-tuned to do special work and you need to stay in synchronization with us. Please write with us at least every other day to keep the flow open and to rechannel your energies into wider and stronger alliance. There are many changes*

occurring now in and on the material plane. You are aware of the weather patterns errat-ic behavior. More is to come even more per-plexing and hazardous from your perspec-tive as humans. New values will be estab-lished, for what you think important is very frail and fleeting in the larger spiritual per-spective. Humanity has much to learn and much growth is on the way. You will have your share of suffering but will also be in a position to aid and assist others in your community. There is nothing you need do to prepare for this except be willing to write and gradually open more to this type of writ-ing and flow from overshadowing energy sources. Much will change. Others will be struck by new awarenesses and abilities as well. It will be quite a different life from what you can even imagine right now. Very uplifting on one level, very tragic on another for what you trust in your world of material-ity will be fragmented and a new type of trust will need to be established. Part of your work is to cooperate with the higher forces in opening you more fully. These qui-et times are all we can get and we must do this when you are accessible. Now you will sleep a bit. We love you.

I received an e-mail back from Raum on June 21, 2009, which said:

Hi Joan,

I've given 3-10-89 considerable thought and have to say that this particular writing suggests that this source gives the impression as to be an "Elevated One." At least that is what I sense by the language used. I agree that you were/are being "fine-tuned" for use by these Wise Ones and further probing of the nature of this/these channeled entities could certainly bring you closer to the Source. Personally, I would like to hear what more information this channel can provide before completely deciding if it is your higher consciousness in touch with you, or if it is indeed something beyond that ken. Even after all this time has gone on, I think it would be worthwhile to appeal to these forces for further guidance and help.

Thanks for letting me see your work.

Adonai,
Raum

Then on August 25, 2009 during a brief meditation, these words came into my mind: *"We will bring you a dream."* I kind of blew it off because dream recall at that time had been so scant. This message came through a second time, a bit more insistently, so I made a bargain that if I did remember a dream, I would make a conscientious effort to start writing with Them again.

Interestingly, that next morning I recorded two

dreams, one at 3:00 a.m. and the other at 6:00 a.m. The dreams weren't of great significance but the fact that I'd made the agreement and then received *two* dreams made an impression. I began to write again, three times a week.

It's an interesting process. I still am not totally convinced that my own thoughts aren't intermingled in the writings because they seem to be coming from my mind. I think the reality is that the information comes *through* my mind. When I re-read these Guided Writings a day or so later, they sometimes surprise me because I often have no conscious recollection of the material at all. I understand that I receive telepathically yet it does have to function through my mind. My Communicators encourage me to write as quickly as I can so that I stay open to their images/thoughts/words and keep my own thoughts from interfering. The problem with this method comes later when I try to transcribe the scribbling.

The following selections are from 2011, 2012 and 2013 up to the cut-off point for this book. These are excerpts on various topics, which include tips for writing my first book (2011) and suggestions for this present one. You'll notice places where They begin a sentence by saying "Yes." This is because a question has just gone through my mind and, almost simultaneously, I was already writing the answer on the paper. I leave those in for my own reference and have left them in for you, too.

GUIDED WRITINGS

1/7/11

We are here. You have worked very hard and well on your book. Speak with confidence about all that has happened to you. Only when one experiences events can one know that they are real. Speak your truth.

1/25/11

This book opens the door to your mission—speak to people of your journey into spiritual truth which, in good time, will prove your dreams very real and true. Share what you know.

1/30/11

Changes are upon the earth and many of you are to see the end of this age. There is growth that can be achieved in this sort of chaos. Share your life and these dream experiences with others. The Truth is within; that's the secret. The Truth is within each of you.

3/12/11

We are here. Yes, many souls in Japan have gone to the afterlife. Nuclear reactors, so treacherous, will kill and sicken many. This is a major catastrophe which will af-fect the entire earth.

4/21/11

Your lack of exercise will weaken your legs. You do not want that. Please listen and heed our suggestions. You are very much part of a harmonic in this area. We can-not explain more than that. You are playing a part in a harmonic—like a musical chord. You can understand this. You must be able to function in a healthy body. Your age does not matter—your condition does. Exercise! We love you.

On May 2011, *Journey of Dreams—40 Years of Dream Keeping* was published and 100 copies were delivered to my door. I had prepared a 20-minute talk on Dreams in general and the book, and had invitations to speak to various community organizations. At some point I sat down to just re-read my actual book and the odd dreams seemed to command my attention. There was something unsettling about them, as though they might be real in some way. I didn't want to contemplate something like that and pushed the thought to the back of my mind.

Nothing about this was mentioned in any of the Guided Writings during this period. Spring turned to summer and there were many other things to occupy my mind. A beloved old pet cat had to be put to sleep. There were various other issues, some concerns in the close family and an unexpected death in the extended family. We adopted two four-month-old sibling kittens and on August 23 experienced two earth tremors which were felt up and down the east coast. Then in late September, the Guided Writing had a surprise . . .

9/24/11
We are here. You will write another book. We will help you with it when the time comes. You are exhausted and not remembering dreams because you are very overtired. Please lie down for 30 minutes every afternoon; a daily rest is necessary now.

This was my first awareness that I would have to

write *another* book!

11/6/11

We are here. Yes, you will *be writing another book. There will be major crises in the world and personal events to deal with. Keep moving forward despite all the stresses and upsets. We are closer than you can even imagine.*

11/16/11

Your dreams have not stopped. You can't remember them because you need as much sleep as you can get now. Five hours a night is not enough and if you are in-terrupted to write dreams there is even less sleep. How-ever, you asked for a message and it is to proceed with your speech. *People are becoming more interested; they may not all believe but you will open a few eyes and minds. There will be interesting feedback on the speech. Take heart and get moving with your* next *book.*

My speech topic was 'Were the Mayans Cor-rect?' I gave this seven-minute speech on December 6, 2011 to the local Toastmasters Club which I had joined in order to learn to comfortably speak in public about the topics in my book. The main points of that speech were: Earth is going through a geological event; her changes are affecting all life and events upon her. Nu-clear testing above and below ground has caused great damage and brings threats of quakes and other disasters. Sightings of UFOs are becoming more numerous; ETs have been visiting and watching over Earth for millions of years. We are not alone. Surely something is coming to a climax but when it will happen only God knows;

the rest of us will have to wait and see.

A few comments from other members were "A very interesting topic." "You had everyone's attention!" "Very informative!" "Gripping!"

11/23/11
We are here. You feel tingling on your scalp and palms. This is energy being sent to you—tuning energies within you. You require these links for your work. This information may be put in your new book. It will be published before the final thrust of energy.

1/13/12
(This next comment came the evening after one of my Dream Talks)

You discovered that not everyone is really interested in dreams especially if it requires writing them down. Get started on your next book. You will be helped.

3/3/12
We are here. Your next book should begin where Journey of Dreams *left off in the spring of 2010. Go forward with new things that have occurred, tied in with new dreams. Include any that feel prophetic. Re-read all your old dreams. There will be new developments and revelations in your own life. This next book should be out in 2014. Yes, you will need technical help again.*

I had my marching orders but I didn't know what the book was to be about. Some old dreams and a few new ones from the past two years surely couldn't be interesting enough for an entire book.

3/12/12
Pray for someone to break the secrecy and prove to the world that we are here to help the planet and humanity.

This comment indicates to me that the Beings who write with me are indeed what we call Extraterrestrials!

4/28/12
We are here. There will be many changes in the Earth. Some are the planet's evolutionary shifting; other catastrophes will be caused by humans. The changes affect everyone.

Browsing through my local used bookstore one day in early May, an old paperback caught my attention. It was *UFO Abductions in Gulf Breeze.* I bought it and read it in four sittings.

5/26/12
Yes, you are now sure you have been abducted in your sleep; sometimes a partial sleep. This was one of the reasons for your book! There were other dreams that you overlooked but the many in your book are excellent.

It took a year from the publication of that book for me to actually realize and finally accept that this was true.

6/15/12
We are here. There are many varieties of exoterrestrial

life—some within the earth itself. We are alien to you, yet we are all part of the same great Creative Energy which you call God.

6/25/12
We are here. Yes, your dreams lately take you back in time and to young ages and familiar places. Just record them; you will be using many of these for another book. No, that has not been put on the shelf; you are *to write more. You will have help with the next one. Wait for your co-author to appear. There is much yet in store for your life. We love you.*

6/30/12
Yes, you descend from an exoterrestrial race. If something is to result from this knowing, there will be confirmation of it. Your book holds markers for those who study this. Continue your good diet and keep hydrated.

7/6/12
When you are not actually thinking, you are listening. Begin to do conscious *listening for thoughts which do not originate from your own mind. Discern us, our slightly different voice in your mind. This is good practice for your work to come. This is all. We love you.*

7/20/12
You will recall all the unconscious information you have been given at the time you need it. You are not alone here as a messenger; there are many others. You will all be guided much more directly and consciously then, than you are now.

7/27/12
You are studying very hard in your world and ours. Of course you leave your body every night. If you have no dreams to remember it is because the work you are doing is not meant to be remembered. You notice how your dream elements match or are very similar to those of others you are reading about. You are indeed one of the Star People. All will be made clear at some point in your lifetime.

8/3/12
Continue reading; one book leads to another. Investigate similar books on the internet also. Soon the ET and UFO interest will begin to peak and the disinformation from the media will not prevail. Once the belief and proof is out and confirmed by millions of people, there will be a new energy in the world; a new sense of hope.

I learned how to find and buy used books on the internet, which opened up a new world to me. I prefer paperbacks because I like to jot down page numbers and make notes inside the covers and in page margins. My little office began to turn into a library.

8/10/12
We are here. You will find others who are working in their own ways to advance the percentage of believers and bring about the evolutionary step upwards. Speak your Truth. You know it now. There are numerous examples in your book. You did not realize this when you included them. You have been spared remembrance of the testing. If you want to know more you can be regressed. You are a contactee now.

10/10/12

We are here. Yes, we have had you aboard our craft many times. You have dreams of these experiences, some quite recently. You were not surprised to know you have been and still are being visited at night and also visiting us. Yes, you don't remember; that is best. You need to live and thrive in your earth life.

This autumn I had three biofeedback sessions. I was hooked up to a computer via straps around my head, wrists and ankles. The computer gives feedback on various systems of the body. Because I had told the owner/operator of my interests I was invited to have a special programming at the end of my sessions. I could ask questions that my subconscious would respond to by indicating a positive or negative reaction on the computer. Some of my questions and the responses are listed below:

Have I really been contacted by extraterrestrials?
Yes

Is this contact still continuing?
Yes

Are any of my spiritual guides angels?
No

Is my primary guide, my Unseen Companion, an ET?
Yes

Should I trust my dreams?
Yes

Am I really supposed to write another book?
Yes

10/17/12
If you want to know your past history with us and others you will need to find a hypnotist. When it's time, one will turn up for you. Don't be too anxious.

1/4/13
Life will not be easy for anyone. Try to stay out of the emotional stressors. Drink more water! Much more! We love you. Please do what you can to keep in good health. You need to stay hydrated. This is very important.

On the night of January 10, I woke up barely able to breathe and feeling horrible. I couldn't swallow anything without choking. Eric took me to my doctor's office as soon as it opened. He took one look at me and said, "You get over to the emergency room right now!"

I stayed all day in one of the emergency room cubicles because the hospital had no available beds. The flu was epidemic. I was rehydrated, given blood tests, antibiotics and discharged to home that evening. It was the "A-strain" flu which wasn't included in the flu shot I got in September.

2/1/13
We are here. You have had a long siege of illness. It was necessary to be immunized at this time against this virus and other components within it. You have been getting a lot of rest, have you not? Yes, it was enforced but it has been an interesting experience for you to be

64

laid-back, literally—*napping and resting. The NFL channel has been helping you; its characters are strong, healthy specimens and this has psychologically fed your flagging energies. See on Sunday if the Ravens win.*
(They did win the Super Bowl.)

2/14/13
We are here. You are in training and have been for a long time. You will be an aid and help to many people in your area. It will all come about in an orderly progression. You have been carefully guided for many years. Do not doubt. Keep speaking to your club. Let your speeches go out to be shared. This is part of your mission. You are a messenger, a go-between.

3/4/13
When you are not incarnate, you too, are an extraterrestrial. For your next speech you will have guests; this will start the ball rolling.

4/6/13
We are here. Let us establish a weekly meeting to communicate together. You may take the weekends off. Yes, you smile. We love you and thank you for your dedication to your dreams these many years as well as the time you presently spend on the old journals, searching for a clue to reveal what your next book is to be about. You will get more information when you are ready to find the focus. Steady progress through all the previous dreams will turn up gems. Be patient and all will be tied up neatly at the proper time.

On March 10 I gave a speech titled "Have You Been Contacted?" This was my publisher, Karen Mireau's, first night at Toastmasters. After the meeting she came over to me and said that her aunt had been abducted. We chatted for awhile and she gave me one of her business cards. It turned out that she owns her own publishing company and had just moved to North Carolina from California. A few weeks later we met for lunch and I asked her to publish my book. The comment by my Guides on March 4 was right; my speech surely did start the ball rolling!

4/18/13

We are here. We cannot force ourselves upon you. Humanity must be willing to allow us to come in peace. This many not happen soon enough. The Earth cannot tolerate much more abuse. Calamity comes this year from natural forces of nature but also terrible deeds by crazed individuals.

5/8/13

Your next book will evolve gradually and then you will discover the purpose. It will be a timely, useful and successful book. It will suddenly all come together. More dreams and writings will be added to help point the way. In our world your book is already written but in your world you must go through all the steps to create it. Let Karen help you; that's why she's here now.

Can you imagine what it's like to be told to write a book and not know what it's to be about? I was reading others' books, taking notes of things that were of interest but feeling like a ship without a rudder.

5/24/13

Yes, buying nose/mouth breathing masks is a good idea. They will come in very useful in the future anyway but when you notice these fragmented cloud patterns, there surely are chemicals from the planes spraying in the atmosphere. The air is not safe to breathe. Take some photos with your camera.

I went out for a walk the next day with my camera and looked up at the sky from the street in front of my house. Amazingly, there was a plane in the process of spraying! I took several photos of it and the sky during my walk.

Chemtrails

Among the various topics I came across in my reading were several Native American prophecies. Prominent among the ones on the internet is a Hopi Prophecy that states: **'The sky will become so dirty that it will cause diseases which will become worse and worse.'**

Another Hopi Prophecy says that they will know the great cleansing and upheaval of Mother Earth is near when they '**see roads crisscrossing the continent like a spider web.**' If these "roads" are in the skies, it seems that the time the prophecies warn us about has already arrived in the form of chemtrails.

5/26/13
We wanted to see if you would do as we asked and write on a non-week night. You got the message and we gave you information that will be helpful. So we are satisfied that we're on the same page. Yes, a bit of humor for you.

6/5/13
Many people around the world are dying now and there will be a great many more. Let us not dwell on what cannot be changed. Just know that these souls contracted to come into this life and to leave it at their appropriate times. It is no accident when someone dies.

6/17/13
You have a connection to the stars—most people do. Yours is somewhat unique.

7/4/13
We are here. This book is excellent for you to judge your own experiences against. There are many markers for you to know that you have been abducted, borne hybrids and are a contactee with many messages and much information in your subconscious waiting to be triggered and released into your consciousness. When that time comes it will be very much a shock to you but

you will understand when it happens.

The book I was currently reviewing was *Alien Jigsaw* by Katharina Wilson. When I first read this book I sent a letter to the author c/o the publisher as directed on a back page. It was returned to me, "Unknown."

7/12 /13
We are here. Your book needs to contain your knowledge and truth. You have read a great many books and found significant events and experiences of others which match your own, already published in your first book. Those are your verifications, your truths. We taught you to leave your sleeping body easily and naturally and come to meet those of us who are guiding and teaching you. You have had many adventures with us and are continuing to do so even though you don't remember most of them.

8/7/13
We are here. The Earth is dying and this cannot go on. No one knows what will happen. We are watching carefully. If there is a cataclysm, whether caused by Earth, by humans or by nature, we will rescue the Star People. It is an unsettling situation. Put your precognitive dreams of future possible events in the book. This book will be a simple, straightforward story with clear dreams proven to be prophetic and with the ring of truth.

8/22/13
We must save this planet. We would like also to save this civilization but we truly do not know if this will be

possible. Mankind may set off a nuclear explosion or
cause a catastrophic accident and put itself asunder.
It has happened before and could happen again.

9/6/13
Sleep for you is very important indeed; if you do not get
enough sleep, you will not remember your dreams. It
behooves you to dream. Then we can send information
to you that you will know does not originate in your
own mind but comes through it. You are a dreamer.
This is why you chose this mind, body, birth date and
time. There is a purpose—and dreams are a major focus
for you and your mission. This is enough writing for to-
night. We love you.

On September 24 at a Toastmasters area contest, I
chatted with the wife of one of the other members and
mentioned my book. I told her there would be one more
book after this one but that I'd first need to find a hypnotist. Immediately she gave me the name of one who
lives here in town. What a timely message this was!

9/24/13
We are here. Yes, you have the name of a hypnothera-
pist—exactly what you are looking for, right in your
own town. Was this guided? Of course it was! You had
the right conversation with the perfect person at a sig-
nificant moment in time. A coincidence? Not at all. Do
you like the way you are so gently guided?

10/29/13
Information will come to you in flashes of inspiration
that you need to write down immediately. You cannot

expect to remember these details with so many things on
your mind.

10/30/13

*The world is close to losing this civilization of humanity
to sheer greed and stupidity. Move on with your book; it
does need to be written. Next year will bring big change
and challenge. You have several excellent prophetic
dreams in the process which will garner attention.
Move forward as quickly as you can on the book.*

12/13/13

*You may uncover unpleasant things under hypnosis but
you can deal with it; it's all in the past. You are strong
after all these years. You'll learn what you need for a
realistic third book about the truth behind your abduc-
tion/contact scenario. We love you and your willingness
to do this mission. You have great courage.*

"Dreams must be heeded and accepted,
for a great many of them come true."

Philipus Aureolus Paracelsus
German Physician
(c.1493 - 1541)

CHAPTER FOUR

Dream Potpourri:

Message Dreams
Precognitive Dreams
Special Dreams

MESSAGE DREAMS

Messages come by mail, telephone and in person. When you ask a question and receive an answer, that's a message, too. If you're concerned or wondering about something—how, why, when, who—and then, surprisingly, the answer comes to you via TV, the internet, in a book or newspaper—that's a message. The dream world also sends messages. You may *see words* clearly written out in front of you or *hear a voice* speaking distinctly.

Message dreams are usually remembered because they're sent specifically to get the attention of your conscious mind. Whenever you wake with a message, immediately write down *exactly* what you have just read or heard. Even though the information may not make sense at the moment, at a later time—days, weeks, months or even years later—you will understand it. I've had messages that came true as quickly as that same day—and as long as eleven years later. Not all messages are personal; some are general, some need thought or contemplation, as you'll notice in a few of the samplings of my dreams.

If recording your dreams seems like too much work—and it does take dedication—you'd be well-advised to at least write down any message dreams you have. They come to get your attention, to give warnings, advice, important information and answers to questions you ask. Make the effort to periodically read them over again. You'll be surprised at how accurate and helpful these messages are.

There's an old dream that begins the selection of these message dreams. I came across it while re-reading all my old dreams searching for the most pertinent for this book. In 1983 I didn't understand this message. Now, I believe I do.

3/13/83

I vividly recall reading a full 8 x11" typewritten page about "Kings." The sheet is loose but seems to be part of a longer work or book. It's somewhat gray with black type. I read it clearly, rapidly and with full comprehension. The gist of it is that there were about 520 Kings, highly evolved Spiritual Beings, who had in times long past been much closer to humanity. Now, however, humanity has become so contaminated that it is practically impossible for any of these Kings to get through to us.

I understood that "Kings" referred to superior, divinely endowed Beings who were called Avatars. All religions have had outstanding spiritual figures who lived among humanity, teaching, preaching and enlightening. Whatever else I read and understood within the dream experience was not allowed to come back to my consciousness. I think this message is well suited for this book which, They tell me, will be published and read during chaotic times.

1/29/84

There is and always will be a particular male with me. I'm allowed to know this now. He appears to be about 30 years old but is a very "old soul." Although I don't recognize him, I understand that I have

76

known him for a long, long time.

This was an unusual message combining an image of some sort with information telepathically impressed on my mind. I have no recollection of actually *seeing* this Being. I believe this is a special Guide, my Unseen Companion or perhaps my Star Guardian.

9/18/10 - 2:32 a.m.
"Oh, everybody *loves* Valrami!" (val <u>ray</u> mi) **I've just heard a female voice say this very expressively and definitively. No visual image or anything else accompanies the voice but immediately I understand that this is important and I wake up.**

The previous afternoon I had been reading about dreams and the fact that many guides don't have names; they're known in the spiritual dimension by their vibrations. Before sleeping, I asked: Does my guide have a name he could spell or express? This little message was my answer.

12/31/10 - 5:30 a.m.
A very young girl, about 3 or 4 years old, says in a high, piping little voice, "He's trying to get serious in his liver." She makes this sound as though it's an admirable endeavor. I don't know to whom she's referring or where I am. There are a few nebulous figures nearby and we all realize that she's trying to say cirrhosis of the liver.

This short dream needs no explanation. This message, from the mouth of a babe, is clear. Because it's my dream, I'm the one who must determine who "he" is. That remains to be seen.

1/27/11

There's a shower area in a camp-style bath house with cinder block cubicles and shower curtain openings. As I enter, a pleasant slightly younger woman greets me. She's very lively, talkative and joyful and appears to be covered from head to toe in glistening white soap bubbles! She tells me things, gives me information that I need to know as well as some instruction. I hold my hands out toward her as I take this all in.

The message here, illustrated symbolically, is that a white-garbed Teacher imparted wisdom and guidance during my sleep. If our conscious minds were allowed to know everything that occurs in the spiritual dimensions it would interfere with our daily lives. I've had many dreams where information is sent directly into my subconscious mind and been alerted to this fact.

2/24/11

I'm staying in a small one room mobile trailer. From time to time a man comes in; he's a friend or helper, perhaps my boss. He oversees me and my work and we travel together. He sleeps in a tent-like area in the side of this trailer and zips himself in. He's quite clever, easy-going and great fun to have around. I enjoy being in his presence!

78

Before going to sleep I asked to see one of my guides. This small one-room mobile trailer is a symbol for my physical body. "Overseeing" my work surely sounds like a guide. These clever symbols and metaphors are indicative of the sense of humor in the spiritual realms. I asked to see a guide; my answer or message was perceptive, but not visual.

4/12/11 - 5:00 a.m.
I float or hover above a long white table where youthful figures are standing. Each has a small group of alphabet letters before him or her, which spell out words. The entire sentence is readable from my elevated perspective. Some of these letters, especially the i's, need repair. Over time the small slivers of glass, stone or whatever the mosaic designs are comprised of have either deteriorated or dislodged out of place. I sense that these are ancient. This information will be needed in the very near future. I'm helping to oversee the repair to bring it back to perfection so it can be more easily read. Together these letters and words form a message which will be of great importance and will be seen and read by many people.

I could read the message in the dream but wasn't allowed to remember it when I woke. Maybe it was in English because I remember noticing that at least one free-standing 'i' was very much needed.

A very short and similar dream scene followed:

I'm with adults now, part of a group which is assembled in a large circular formation. There's a paragraph—a long message or statement connected with this scene.

I have a feeling that this dream scene will actually occur in some way, revealing an ancient message which will be discovered and prove to be quite amazing.

Two dreams on the same night with the same theme serve to reinforce the information so that it gets through to the consciousness. These are actually pre-cognitive dreams *about a message.*

7/9/11 - 4:00 a.m.
It's bright daylight and I'm alone in the car of a passenger train. There are no controls here; I'm definitely the passenger. To my right is a shiny silvery train, larger than the one I'm in and much more powerful. I don't see any tracks but I know these two trains are running side by side. The other train has the capacity to go at a much faster rate than it's moving now but it's maintaining a speed which allows me to travel along beside it. I am moving at the maximum speed possible for the ability which I have at this time. There is a destination for this trip but I don't know what it is. I have a sense of achievement in my personal progress as I realize that I'm being allowed to comprehend this information now.

The final sentence is my message. This is a progress report. I know that my Star Guardian is the other train—if there even were trains. I believe my subconscious mind created these symbols for me to understand speeding through space in my astral form. Even though I seldom become lucid in my out-of-body dreams, it's exciting when I wake and understand some of the things I've been doing during the night.

2/14/12 – Here's another example of two dreams with the same theme on the same night.

#1. Time not recorded
There are five or six other girls who seem like former high school classmates of mine and we all appear to be about that age. We're each traveling separately to a predetermined place where we'll meet. The roads I'm gliding over are familiar because of their pattern and intricacy. They're short roads with many sharp turns requiring slow but steady progress. I definitely remember this complex place! It's a beautiful, bright sunny day and I sense that this location is an elevated, spacious area which might soon overlook the ocean. Maybe our destination is a vacation at the beach. In spite of the tedious travel, my spirits are high because I know we're quite close to our goal and I have a lighthearted, joyous feeling throughout this journey.

#2. 5:45 a.m.
I'm with four other young women or girls on a mission of some sort with a very definite destination in mind. We make our way stealthily through different neighborhoods and people's yards. As I move past one yard I'm surprised to see a well-kept gravestone

which reads DESMOND or something very similar. We pass two more houses along the way and in front of the third house is another headstone carved with the same name, DESMOND. We're hurrying along rapidly now because it's important that we reach our destination and do what we set out to do. That name or word stays prominently in my mind.

In reality, former classmates of mine are now in their mid-seventies, yet we don't appear that way on the astral/spiritual plane. The second dream has one or two less young women and, in reality, two of my former classmates have passed on. Both dreams are focused on moving toward a goal or destination. Twice, a word similar to Desmond calls attention to itself. In French, the word *monde* is world. *Des* generally means of or from. I've puzzled long and hard about this word DESMOND, which I know is a marker for the message in this dream.

Here's my thought: the gravestones are markers; these particular markers stand out for attention. I believe that *des mond(e)* indicates that the graves of mankind are the markers of our physical deaths on earth. The goal or pre-determined destination is the spiritual realm where there is no death. A vacation at the beach is a positive symbol in my dreams. The brightness and joyousness indicate that these dreams are taking place in a spiritual dimension. We have to hurry because (in reality) we're not 'spring chickens!'

2/24/12 - 4:45 a.m.
"The people of the earth will know beyond the shadow of a doubt that something is truly going

82

wrong with the planet and forces of nature."

This message was very clear in my mind as I woke suddenly. Its interpretation is open to everyone. My personal thought is that Earth is a living entity and goes through cycles in its evolutionary process. Mankind has not taken good care of the planet. When the natural rhythms and processes of the Earth are interfered with the planet suffers; this causes the suffering of all living forms upon the planet. Previous civilizations destroyed themselves by misusing weapons of war and abusing technological information and knowledge. Present humanity is following dangerous practices as well, in our abuse of the planet and each other.

11/9/12 - 4:45 a.m.
The scene is a large junior high school where I'm a substitute or a new teacher here this year. Someone has just told me that I'm in charge of the annual production this year. The first meeting is at the end of school today. I've never done anything like this before nor seen the annual production. How did I get into this situation? The frustration and inner turmoil wakes me.

Schools represent learning experiences and I've been handed a huge assignment. With 20/20 hindsight a year later, I know this message refers to this second book which reveals that some of my dreams are memories of abductions and ongoing contacts with extraterrestrial aliens. Inner turmoil indeed!

12/1/12

At a gasoline station somewhere, I've been given three choices: I can fill, watch or wait. This seems strange—it's an unfamiliar way of doing things. There are many other people around this area who are quiet and simply observing. I confer briefly with someone in a small group near me. There are no voices used—I focus my attention and telepathically exchange information with this person whom I don't see. I opt to be in the group or category that will be watchers.

I really don't know what this message means. Of the three choices offered, I chose to *watch.* I asked for input from someone nearby in order to make this decision. The symbolism indicates jobs or work options— one active, one semi-active and one inactive.

3/6/13 - 3:15 a.m.

There is somewhere I'm supposed to be going or something important I need to do. Two or three Energies nearby are encouraging me to be ready. I don't see them but I can *feel* their presences. I seem to be sluggish—a bit confused and overwhelmed by many distractions. I *do* want to cooperate and seriously attend to what they are urging me to do but I don't seem to have much stamina right now.

This dream was elusive! It came and went as I lay there not able to wake up quite enough to write it down at 3:00 a.m. After having the flu in early January, I struggled for six months to regain my strength and energy. Sleeping poorly was another problem during this long period. What I was supposed to be doing was writing a second book and I didn't know *why*!

8/9/13 - 3:00 a.m.
Immediately after performing a specific feat, the dreamer is required to put in a number and then repeat the feat for verification. If it cannot be duplicated within the same time frame it is negated as false and may not be recorded that it was accomplished at all. This rule or law is very frustrating to me because it's difficult in *this* mental state to duplicate what was done in the enhanced state I was in when first performing the feat, whatever it was.

There was testing of some sort which I (and probably everyone) must undergo. The rules were explained in this short dream with a firm message. I understood them perfectly within the dream reality. The work seemed to involve a mental repetition and remembrance. As I woke slightly and realized I'd been dreaming, I understood the fantastic concept of the requirement. That other reality doesn't 'give an inch' no matter what the circumstances! The message here is: **Perform your very best every time or none of it will count!**

That evening, the Guided Writing had a comment:

> *"There were two dreams but you recalled only one. Yes, the tests in the higher realms are difficult but when you succeed it truly means something. You got the gist of that dream."*

9/17/13 - 1:15 a.m.

I'm walking through a large hotel corridor on an upper level. It's a wide circular hallway which seems slanted, like a spiral. I'm moving upward on the left side and there may be windows on this left wall. I pass and greet people who are coming down from the opposite direction, all of them strangers to me. Even though I don't know them, I make it a point to be friendly and give each a smile of total acceptance and harmony. No matter how different they are from the people most of us have been used to seeing, we must be kind and gracious to all. I feel great joy and elation throughout the dream.

It was very windy during the night and the awnings over the partially open French doors were flapping somewhat loudly. This frightened the cats; they woke me and I recalled this dream which has a good message for all of humanity—**no matter how different someone may look, be kind and gracious to everyone**. It is possible that this dream experience took place in a large UFO and that these "different" people were members of various ET races from other dimensions.

9/27/13 - 2:30 a.m.

On a beautiful day somewhere, I'm on a golf course with a group of men. Dad is one of them and he's much younger than I've ever seen him! I feel like "one of the guys" here except there is no interaction between any of them and me. They don't even know that I'm here. Later, I walk over to where Dad is pruning a large flowering shrub. Just before I reach him, he answers a call on his

cell phone. The person on the phone tells him that someone he knows has died.

The dream ended at this point. As an unseen observer, I saw the young spiritual form my father has chosen to take in that dimension. He enjoyed working in the yard but the odd marker here is that my father never had a cell phone. This is a clue to the message —someone he knows has died.

I have to wonder whether this is a new twist to the family omen dream. (In my mother's family for several generations, a deceased member pays a visit to the dreamer and fairly soon afterwards, someone in the family passes on.) Time will tell whether or not this was an unusual precognitive second-hand message.

12/4/13 - 6:25 a.m.
A good friend and I, both of us young, are somewhere in an antiquated building watching an old movie we saw long ago when we were kids. This is taking place in the upper level of a warehouse or storage area. Many television sets are lined up in a long row along old wood plank floors. This movie we're being allowed to watch features three young women. We're particularly interested in seeing them again and I understand that it's a special privilege for us to be allowed to see this old film.

Now later, I've been given a telepathic message that it's time to go. I feel myself being quickly moved backwards to the end of the aisle of TVs. Then I'm turned and begin to slide in another direction, as

though in a little car on an amusement park ride. Smoothly and rapidly I slide forward until I hear my female cat meow. Immediately I come to a stop in my bed without any discomfort or dizziness. I'm very much aware that I've just left a place where I was lively and alert and am now here, where I feel dull, heavy and groggy with sleep.

Angie jumps up onto the bed. I bring my arm from under the covers and reach out to touch her soft, warm fur. I open one eye and peer at the clock; the green digits read 6:25 a.m. It's an hour later than the usual wake-up meow. I turn on the small electric candle, then put the clipboard beside my pillow and begin to record this dream. It's exciting to have the experience of these two different dimensions to describe! I slide a foot out from under the covers to indicate my intention to get up. Gabby's cold nose touches my toes. The cats will have to wait a few more minutes for breakfast.

Gabby and Angie

Four-month-old siblings Gabby and Angie joined our family on August 1, 2011. They're delightful companions to us and to each other. The cats have olive-colored eyes and gray fur which has a silvery sheen in sunlight and camera flash. One or both sleep on my bed—but only when I'm in it. They determine when it's time for me to get up in the morning, whether 4:15, 5:00 or, if I'm lucky, 5:30. I've learned that 9:00 p.m. is a good time to go to bed.

I continue writing and try to assess the feeling of *who* I am in this dream; I was vitalized with energy, animated, vigorous and, therefore, I *felt* young. I never saw this good friend and consciously I have no idea who she might be other than a delightful buddy in the spiritual world. The best way to understand and explain who I am in this dream is, simply, that I am *me. My spiritual essence is ageless, ongoing and eternal.*

I'm sure that sliding rapidly back to my bed is the process of returning through the astral cord to my physical body. I've never felt the sensation quite like this before. I was swiftly and unerringly returned to my physical body from the astral state.

The message of this dream is the experience at the end. When you need to wake up, you'll glide right back into your body! I believe my Guidance gave me this dream for you, the reader of this book. They said that I would find 'gems' among my dreams and this one *feels* like a gem!

PRECOGNITIVE DREAMS

There's a distinction between the terms precognitive and prophetic. Precognitive dreams suggest that something *may* happen in the future. They're like rehearsals of events that could possibly play themselves out. Prophetic dreams, like the Biblical prophecies, predict or forecast what *will* come to pass in the future.

Everyone rehearses scenarios during sleep before the scenes play themselves out upon the three-dimensional stage of our human dramas. Edgar Cayce, the "Sleeping Prophet," who was in touch with a very high spiritual level during his sleep-induced trances, firmly believed that nothing happens to us in our lives that we haven't first experienced in a dream. I have published dreams which played themselves out in reality; therefore in *retrospect*, I know that some of my dreams are prophetic. At the time of a dream however, I don't know whether or not it will come into manifestation. Sometimes a particular dream just *feels* different in some way, which is difficult to explain. One dream may be entirely devoid of feeling while another is full of emotion—but upon waking, I usually have a *sense* that this dream was no ordinary one. Therefore, I choose to call these dreams possibly precognitive. They're usually of very clear scenes and often I have some insight as to what's happening or the dream makes a strong impression on my mind in some way. I note these feelings for the record in my dream journals.

I must have been working on the selection of these dreams in early August, because on the evening of August 9, 2013, the Guided Writing revealed this:

"Your possibly prophetic dreams are very true to life now. Do not be afraid to publish them."

And so they are being published here, although I will continue to call them possibly precognitive until they prove otherwise.

In a previously published short dream on May 6, 1979, I remarked to someone after we'd felt mild shaking of the cottage: "Even though they say we don't get earthquakes around here, we're definitely going to get a real big one someday." At the time of this dream I was still living in Massachusetts but by the end of that year I had relocated permanently to North Carolina.

On August 23, 2010, the North Carolina Sandhills area had two mild earth tremors. The first was a 5.8 magnitude, the second a little less and was felt up and down the east coast. I was alerted to this by the ten crystals which began to swing and bang loudly against the glass panes of the French door in my office. Then I distinctly felt the slight rocking motion of the room. Fortunately, it wasn't "a real big one" but it surely did get everyone's attention! This particular dream could also be termed a message dream because a clear message was voiced—my own voice—a peculiarity for my message dreams!

1/2/11 - 5:15 a.m.
I'm taking a summer school course at college.

91

One day while I'm rinsing shampoo out of my hair in the shower, the water pressure suddenly decreases. After opening my eyes to find the faucets, I notice a lot of four-to five-inch strands of dark hair all over my right leg and side; it's fallen off my head!

Unfortunately, this little dream proved to be prophetic. In early January of 2013, I came down with the flu and was hospitalized for a day to be rehydrated. In early March my hair began to fall out; a fifty-cent size mass of dark and silver hair accumulated on the drain after every shampoo. This dire situation lasted into June. The reference to summer school indicates a temporary situation and college suggests an intensive learning experience. After a change of thyroid medication, the addition of whole food supplements and better daily hydration finally slowed my hair loss to near-normal shedding by the end of the year. Water pressure suddenly decreasing is a clue here; I seldom feel thirsty and it didn't occur to me to drink water during the day. I learned the hard way in this case; my hair is thinner now on the crown and right side.

2/23/11
Last evening I asked to know about an event that would come sometime in my future. I woke from this dream at 1:15 a.m.

I'm observing a fascinating scene. It's the arrival of my own newly-arrived soul from this physical lifetime. I've just landed somewhere in great confusion. Part of me feels the landing and these emotions. After a rough few moments of being thrust here very

quickly, I'm caught and handled gently. It takes a bit of time for the several Beings around me, whom I sense and seem to know but don't actually *see*, to get me calmed and settled down.

Now, more awake, I sense that there was an *explosive* event – sudden and violent. If this truly depicts the end of my lifetime, I'll be instantly ejected from my body and never know what hit me. It's very busy here where I've landed. No doubt many other souls have likewise arrived suddenly in the same state of confusion. It's comforting to know I'll be in good hands! Also it's good to know that I won't suffer through a long, drawn-out death. My dream request brings to mind the adage, "Be careful what you ask for . . ."

If this preview of my last moment on Earth is prophetic, then the preparatory information for my memorial service which I have on file at a local funeral home will be for naught. I'm including one especially meaningful item here which is on the list so that it might make a connection with me when I'm in spirit. This is the third verse of an old hymn which was sung fairly often in the church I attended as a young teenager. The last line of the verse so emotionally affected me that I choked up and tears welled in my eyes every time we sang it.

Several years ago I located the hymn in a retired *Pilgrim Hymnal* and memorized that verse. I use it now as the opening for my evening prayers:

"So long Thy power has blessed me—
Surely it still will lead me on
Over moor and marsh, over crag and torrent
Until the night is gone.

And, with the dawn,
Those angel faces smile,
Which I have loved long since—
And lost awhile."

2/26/11 - 5:30 a.m.
I'm on an airplane with President Obama, his wife and their daughters. This plane has landed in a foreign country; a neutral nation in a warm climate area. This is only a temporary stop. They are seeking sanctuary because there's some kind of serious problem. I don't know why I'm here. The latest issue of a large glossy magazine is on my lap. It's called M.O.L. or L.O.M. for short but I can't remember the actual title. The feature article is about the President, his job and family; their photo is on the cover.

The President strolls by and sits down. He's a quiet, aloof person and we don't speak until he notices the magazine. He says, "It's out now, huh?" I hold it up and say, "Yes, but I haven't read it yet." I feel that I should read the article but right now I can't seem to focus enough even to comprehend any of the words. The Obamas are seeking asylum because they're in some sort of danger. There is something furtive involved in this situation. I'm only an observer here. A quiet, serious male is with me, unobtrusively out

94

of sight. He's a mentor to me in some way, very intelligent and supportive.

This was all I recalled of the surprising and possibly precognitive short dream. The protective presence of a Guardian made this dream feel even more important.

3/1/11 - 4:50 a.m.
I'm at an unfamiliar college, sitting in a huge auditorium packed with people. I can't recall why I'm here except that there has been a major upset or situation which has disturbed our lives. We've been herded into this stadium-like place, squeezed in like sardines, and told to stay here. Everyone is tense and restless. Most of the people in this huge crowd are students but there is a large number of people like me and my Unseen Companion—who just happened to be in this area when the unusual and unfortunate event occurred. Apparently we've been brought here for our safety. None of us will be allowed to leave until the people in charge let us go.

There was an oppressive feeling of dread and tension throughout the dream. I had no sense of where we were or who was in charge and I woke with the feeling that something like this *could* happen.

3/10/11
There's a small rural grocery store where I'm pushing a shopping cart through a few aisles. The packaged food items are scarce and the produce unappealing. There are only two or three other shoppers

here and we all seem to be psychologically depressed and unhappy. I don't know why.

Life as we once knew it had changed. There were no other clues or feelings to offer about this short scene except that I hope that it doesn't come to pass.

4/9/11

There's a play that I was in once before. I don't know what the play is but I seem to be filling in at the last moment. There haven't been any rehearsals and I don't know why; in fact nothing seems clear except that I'm definitely involved in this performance.

Now backstage, I'm quickly changing into my first costume. The play has already begun but I'm not quite ready! I check my hair in a mirror—or maybe I'm able to step outside of myself to look at my hair —and I'm shocked at what I see. My hair is very thin and my scalp looks bright pink and irritated. I call out in dismay, "Oh no! I'm losing my hair!" This is horrifying to me.

This was my second dream about hair loss, which would actually begin in March, two years into the future! It's been interesting to read these dreams again and see how incidents in my life were being laid out in front of me. Even knowing this, how could I have prevented it? I had the flu shot in September but got the flu anyway and it took a toll on my body and health. My dream life suffered also because I wasn't remembering many of them. I understood that I needed the sleep but missed the dreams. Then I noticed that they conveniently began to come about the time the cats would normally be waking me up in the mornings.

These next four dreams are in a grouping because they're related. Each is precognitive for the same event which would occur within two months from the date of this first dream in the series:

6/15/11 - 5:50 a.m.
I've gone to Mom's for lunch. The house is unfamiliar to me. Mom isn't in the kitchen so I call out to her but get no response. I hear the sound of the TV and, when I enter that room, I immediately know by the look on Mom's face that there's a problem. Then my grandmother steps out from where she's been sitting. I'm surprised to see her and notice an odd expression on her face also. There's definitely something amiss; one or the other has bad news.

The dream ends, reminding me of the family "omen dream"—when a deceased member of the family comes to visit, a family member will soon die.

7/11/11 - 3:30 a.m.
My grandmother has come to visit me. She moves around the room engaged in lively conversation. I remember nothing except that she's here.

This was the second visitation from a deceased family member in less than a month. Surely, a message was being delivered to my consciousness. Even though I was very much aware of the family omen, no clues were revealed.

8/8/11 - 5:00 a.m.
**A jolly woman has just informed me that Mary or-
dered a cheese party platter and put it in the trunk
of my car. There's pleasant camaraderie with some
friends in a wooded rural area near a small delica-
tessen. These five or six people, whom I never quite
see, are relatives and friends of "Pete's" family. Apparently they haven't seen each other in a long time
and this is a joyous mini-reunion by coincidence at
the deli. However, I sense there's a reason why we're
all buying food here.**

Currently my first husband, "Pete," is in a Ten-
nessee hospital with a sudden illness. Our sons are both
there and keeping me informed of the situation. His
condition is worrisome and the doctors don't know
what's wrong.

8/10/11
**In an unfamiliar school location at the end of the
day, someone calls out to me, "Your husband died."
That jolts me for a moment until I recall that Pete
has been in a hospital. Then I remember that he's
my *former* husband and that I'm married to "Eric"
now. I'm confused and ask, "Which one?" There's
no response.**

About 9:20 on the morning of August 12, 2011,
my son Rob called to tell me, "Dad passed away early
this morning." Later, we learned that the cause of death
was a ruptured aneurysm under the back part of the

aorta where it attaches to the heart. Evidently in the spiritual world, once married, that person is always part of the family. This coming event was announced in three *prophetic* dreams and one direct *message* dream. When the subconscious wants to get information to the conscious mind, it will keep presenting the message in different ways until it gets through. (Pete had an older cousin named Mary, who, it appears, has passed on.)

When *Journey of Dreams* was published in May, one of my sons told Pete about it and he bought a copy on Amazon. After reading it, Pete phoned me. He wanted me to know that he had "no issues with it." He said that everything I had written about him was the truth. This surprising revelation prompted me to apologize for my shortcomings as a wife. In turn, he apologized for his transgressions during the marriage. In that brief exchange, it felt as though we cleared the past. After Pete's death this conversation came back to me like a signal that the last piece of a puzzle had been put into place.

8/18/11 - 5:30 a.m.
I'm standing in a depressed area, both literally and figuratively. My surroundings appear to be a large, low-lying barren stretch of land which is being used as a campground of some sort. I'm surrounded by tent-like shelters. This unpleasant place has a somber ambience. I've just learned that there's a new rule or law here: anyone who wants to fly the flag must get permission and pay a fee to do so. These flags are not actually "flown" however; they're small flags on sticks that may be stuck into the

ground beside the shelter where we live. They're American flags!

As I struggle to comprehend this, I feel shocked! Where *am* I? What's happened here? I think I'm still in the southern United States in a huge deserted area—except for all these tents. Where are the trees? As I look farther out, I see that we're surrounded by a metal fence! This situation is very difficult to understand and I wake feeling emotionally overwhelmed.

This dream felt like it *could* be precognitive. I pray that it never becomes reality! This was one of several dreams I wish I'd never remembered.

9/9/11 - 4:15 a.m.
Several other adults and I are observing a large group of children in a well-lighted church building. My son Rob is one of them. An announcement is made that he has been singled out to win a prize. Rob goes to the front of the room to claim his prize: "The Little Piggy." It may be a statue of a piglet with tufts of grass around it. It's not clear to me although I do see a little pink piglet sitting outdoors. This is a celebratory gathering and I'm happy for Rob, who is wearing a yellow shirt and appears to be about seven or eight years old. I don't actually *see* anyone else although the room is filled with people.

The bright church setting, joyousness and winning a prize are all very positive symbols. Yellow represents intellect and the ability to think clearly. The award

100

of this piglet is a bit baffling, however.

When I rediscovered this dream in April of 2013, I e-mailed it to Rob and asked if it meant anything to him. It did! He said that his special lady friend has a small piglet mascot that she takes with her on trips and vacations. Rob shared my dream with her and she sent me a photograph of the little pink piggy admiring an ocean view. The young woman and her mascot were not in Rob's life at the time of this dream.

Dream Piggy

10/20/11 - 4:00 a.m.
The scene is a large hotel or apartment house with a temporary college or camp-like feeling. I'm a self-sufficient young adult, living on my own and it's a busy time for me. Someone says that nearly everyone here is getting sick. A germ or virus is spreading through the building. I walk into the large community bathroom and notice that most of the hand soap dispensers are empty. The janitorial staff has been remiss and especially now, the disinfectant soap is needed. Someone suggests that there may be spores

on the cement walls here which are making people ill. I don't want to touch anything but I take two of the empty soap containers off their fixtures and lay them on top of the sinks to attract the attention of the bathroom attendants. This is a worrisome situation.

The "Someone" mentioned is most likely my Unseen Companion who stays with me during many dream experiences and telepathically imparts information about the things I see. This place had a depressive feeling and I was glad to wake up. It is not a stretch of the imagination to believe that germs or viruses could cause a major health problem anywhere in the world.

6/20/12 - 4:00 a.m.
There is to be a downhill endurance race and I'll be participating for the first time. I know it's a winter event because I'm able to project my vision outside and can see a mountain covered with white powdery snow. Somehow this is possible even though I am confined to a bed. My mother is with me in this comfortable although unfamiliar place. She's insisting that I get all the rest I can. I don't actually *see* Mom but I recognize her energy. She's concerned about me because I try to do too much and keep exhausting myself.

I'm already partly dressed in several layers of warm clothing and socks. I want to try on the footwear—something heavy and ungainly—probably ski boots, although I don't see them. Mom won't let me do this so I just lie there and try to relax as we chat tele-

pathically. I'm excited about this upcoming event and, even though I know I won't win this race, all I want is to have the endurance to finish it. This feels like the most important event of my entire life!

My mother passed on in 1979 and was often in my dreams for many years. If this figure was not actually my mother's spirit, it represents a nurturing aspect of myself. This important event is surely my mission in this latter part of my life. I don't think the extraterrestrials will be able to land on Earth during my lifetime but perhaps my efforts can help to prepare the way for them to help humanity and repair the Earth.

In January 2013, (the winter) less than six months after this dream, I was very ill and bedridden with the flu. Hindsight is 20/20 but there were clues sprinkled through the preceding dream. During that illness there was a moment when I realized I *could* die. It seemed to be an option. I chose not to and recovered, although slowly.

In March and April there were four short dreams with similar themes:

3/16/12 - I'm in a hospital somewhere. It's crowded here and things are confused.

3/31/12 - I find myself in an unfamiliar place; it's an old building that's being used as a hospital. I've had some minor procedures done.

103

4/12/12 - I'm just out of the hospital, recovered from whatever my trouble was.

4/19/12 - It's a day or two after I've been admitted to a hospital and I'm recovering. I don't know whether I've been ill or injured.

6/26/12 - The Event

A sudden thunderstorm woke me from a sound sleep at 12:45 a.m. I realized that the windows were open in the sunroom. Still half-asleep, I went downstairs to close the six heavy casement windows. Using both hands, I pushed down the first two windows on the right side of the room. I had just begun to push the third window down when my husband came in to help. Eric said he'd close the rest and told me to go back to bed. As I turned to thank him, I inadvertently removed my left hand from the window but continued to push it down with my right arm. He remembers that I said, "*Ouch!*" and went back to bed.

About 1:30 a.m. I woke suddenly with horrible pain in my right shoulder and chest. I could barely breathe because of the extreme distress in the center of my chest. My pulse was steady and I *knew* it wasn't my heart. I sat up for the rest of the night so that I could breathe a little easier.

In the morning I phoned my doctor's office and was instructed to go to the hospital. Eric drove me to the emergency department. Initially it was thought that I might have a blood clot in my heart but the first group of X-rays and tests ruled that out. I was kept overnight in the Observation Unit—a section of the old hospital building—and had more tests and X-rays the next morning.

On the afternoon of June 27, I was discharged with the diagnosis of a severe strain in my right shoulder and chest muscles. My heart was found to be perfect, two days before my 74th birthday. The hospitalist remarked that this was surprising, considering my age!

1/2/13 - 5:10 a.m.

Something very unusual has happened. There's black murky slime all over the ground here in this unfamiliar outpost-like area. It was discovered quite recently—an eruption, or huge meltdown and leakage—or maybe some sort of oozing from the Earth herself. There are geologists, military, local police and other officials here.

I don't know why I'm here but at this moment I'm trying to walk back to my motel room which is a quarter of a mile away. The slimy stuff is still emerging from its source. I approach a deep trench filled with this thick dark mud and globs of strange orangey goo floating in it. Two investigators dressed in rubbery protective gear are nearby. One of them tells me to be careful and to get back to a safe area. I reply, "That's what I'm trying to do!" Just then I step into a hole and am horrified as the slimy black liquid runs over the top of my right boot and splashes up onto my clothing. Thoroughly frightened now, I hurry through the mire toward the motel.

Now I'm in a public bathroom at the motel, weeping and trying to wipe the icky stuff off my clothing. The more I rub at it, the more it smears and makes a

worse mess. Someone comes to the door and tells me that I have a phone call outside. Still teary-eyed, I go out to where the police and reporters are gathered near a mass of parked cars. I'm handed a cell phone. When I say, "Hello," I hear a man's voice ask for verification that I'm the person he asked to speak to. I reply that I am. Then he tells me his name (his second name begins with a G) and he says, "I was wrong; the substance that we thought was (innocuous) is actually poisonous. Do you understand?" I say, "Yes," and he abruptly hangs up.

I'm stunned. This is a shock which will have devastating repercussions. I can't say anything to these investigators or reporters who are looking at me strangely. I don't know whether the message refers to this muddy slime that has everyone baffled—or if it's about something else entirely. The emotional intensity of this situation abruptly wakes me.

This had all the feelings of a precognitive dream. Some prophetic/precognitive dreams are void of emotion. This one certainly was not and the upset caused me to quickly return to my physical body with a very clear memory of this nightmarish dream.

2/25/13 - 4:20 a.m.
"Microboosha" is strongly in my mind the moment I begin to wake. This is the name of the process or procedure we're using. I've been given a specialized device to hold and use. It's dark-colored and looks metallic although it isn't metal. The shape is somewhat elongated and requires two hands to hold and

106

**use it but it's not heavy. I press or squeeze some-
thing on it and this instrument emits an energy that
sends healing power into a person's body. There's a
line of people waiting to come where I am. I also
sense other forms or people around and behind me.
It seems that I've been trained to use this device to
help people and I'm aware of an awesome emotional feeling while I'm doing it. I'm standing inside an
unusual place; an enclosed area but not a building.
The upper part is rounded and light-colored. I'm
feeling heightened, advanced, super-energized and
unusually intelligent or "tuned in" to my inner core.**

My waking impressions: I've already been
"treated" by or with this device. It heals, cures and
somehow restores the human body to a vibrancy which
is not only sensed by the person receiving it but obvious and visible to others. People who know me have
seen the miraculous change in me. They believe and
trust that they, too, can be revitalized.

I sent this dream to my friend in Massachusetts.
"Raum" responded:

> "The word is micro-booster. You are be-
> ing trained to heal those who come over
> from our side to enter the astral. It is nec-
> essary to revitalize the energy and make
> that soul body whole again. This is a very
> important dream and your Mission here is
> just a learning phase for you in the next
> stage of evolvement."

This was an unusual dream, precognitive to a time which may extend beyond my mortal life. Here are some final thoughts about the situation in this dream. These comments are being enhanced by my ever-present spiritual Guidance:

The Extraterrestrials have created this device for us as proof that they are here to help us. Along with innumerable other humans, I have been trained and taught for many years during sleep to be able to help people who may be frightened of ETs.

A major part of the mission is to let people know that all will be positive. We have nothing to fear from the Extraterrestrial Beings who will be landing on Earth when it is safe for them to do so. They will come in peace.

SPECIAL DREAMS

The ability to recall my dreams and the tenacity and dedication needed to record them has brought an unusual perspective into my life. The following collection of old and recent dreams contains a variety of interesting scenarios and events from various dimensions of the astral and spiritual worlds. Since I've shared so much of my inner life already I'm including these, which are among my favorites.

8/8/71
I'm part of a group of young college students. Each of us has been selected from our various areas for some reason and assembled together in a large auditorium somewhere . . .

This short, simple dream from 43 years ago contains information I understand now, from my present perspective. It refers to my mission in this life as one of the many people who are being educated in "a place of higher learning." At the time of this dream, I had not yet been moved from Massachusetts to North Carolina which is where They chose to place me so that I could fulfill my part in the Plan.

2/4/79 - 5:00 a.m.
The scene is an old-fashioned drugstore/ice cream shop circa 1940. There are young children here, all grammar school ages. As I appear (or discover myself here) some of the youngsters smile, point at me and say, "There she is!" It seems that they have seen me here before and are glad I'm back. Not all of the

children are able to see me, so this is a humorous game I enjoy with those who can. The proprietor of this little shop can't see me either but he plays along with their fantasy about the imaginary lady. These are delightfully happy children. When the perceivers come close to me, they try to touch me and I pretend to reach out to touch them back.

I'm out-of-body in my astral form and only the psychically perceptive children see me. There is no real physical contact when one form is in the astral state. My earthly body is sleeping at home while *I'm* in a reality 70 years in the past. This is an example of Time Travel—another fascinating feature of the dream world.

10/7/83
A 'charge of energy' jolts me! It's accompanied by a flashing explosion in my head which sends out a wave of light-colored smoke and a few sparks. There is no pain.

I was abruptly startled awake during the night by this strange and baffling incident. No ill effects resulted from this anomaly. I would like to think that this energy charge was a positive thing in some way.

5/31/84
I appear—materialize—in a small room directly in front of a sobbing brown-haired boy about nine years old who has been crying over his brother. He's surprised by my sudden appearance and thinks I'm an angel. I console him, speaking softly and giving him a gentle hug. His younger brother is very ill and

lying on a bed to my left side. I try to help him by doing something toward or for the sickly child. Then I abruptly vanish.

I'm aware that I've done healing work in dreams before, so this one didn't surprise me. It's nice to know that I'm able to help others while my physical body sleeps. Recording my dreams has enabled me to discover many things about myself which, otherwise, I wouldn't know. Although it's a different aspect of me who does this work, being aware of it makes the ups and downs of daily life worth living.

2/9/85
The scene is a huge summer camp which seems familiar to me. All of the buildings have the same basic design—they're shiny gray structures with white latticework arches and fences. I seem to know nearly everyone here and it's a joyous reunion.

Camp is a temporary place, the astral dimension. The people in this dream may be the astral forms of humans whose physical bodies are sleeping at home. They also may be the spiritual forms of those who reside in this realm. In either case, I know them and am happy to be visiting here.

6/16/88
It's a lovely evening as I find myself walking somewhere with another girl. There's a mountain in the distance. Everything around me appears alive with vitality—almost magical. The green hues of the foliage are glowing; the very air feels alive with energy

and the sparkling bright stars against the darker sky are stupendous! I stop in my tracks to stare incredulously at this remarkable scene.

This is exactly how the spiritual dimension looks. It's also the way that people who have had near-death experiences describe heaven. It's thrilling to have this kind of adventure during the night and remember it in the morning. I have no fear of death because I know that the *essence* which is *me* will continue on when I leave this physical body for the last time. Spiritual energy is ageless and forever. In this dream I'm a *girl*— not the 50-year-old woman I was in 1988!

7/22/89 - 3:11 a.m.
I suddenly appear in a place where six or seven "Presences of Power" are at a round table or in a circle. There is nothing visible but the sense of strong energies that manifest as radiant lights. To my right is a bright glow of cobalt blue. Beyond that another light is a bright raspberry pink. The other Presences are somewhat different colors but all of equal intensity. This is awesome!

This dream vision lasted only a moment and immediately I woke with the memory. I felt honored to have had this brief glimpse of what I believe are high spiritual level Beings. Whatever the occasion or purpose, it was thrilling to be allowed in their presence and to recall it.

6/13/07 - 3:30 a.m.

There's a group of semi-familiar people at a camp-like place where I may have been before. Right now I'm in my room here and have just noticed two stacks of old letters addressed to me. There are about ten envelopes in this first packet. I don't recall ever seeing these before. My name is clearly written on each one. (I recognize the 'Joan' but don't notice the rest of my name.) **Deep into the second stack and possibly below it is a different letter with a shape and style unlike the others. It's without an envelope, folded intricately and hand-written in an unusual foreign-style penmanship. The color of the ink and design on the paper is pinkish-coral.**

The information in this letter is amazing. It's a prediction of my future which was written for me a very long time ago. I have a vague memory of this but not of who wrote it, when, or why. The letter is comprehensive, spanning from my distant past into the future beyond where I am now. However, my time to read this information is brief and I'm not able to absorb it now. To be allowed the awareness of even a small portion of this document is amazing to me.

It is possible that I was temporarily in an elevated astral state and allowed to see the ancient "Akashic record" of my soul's evolutionary journey. Except for recognizing my name, none of what I read returned to my waking consciousness. Pink-coral indicates spiritual love and, of course, letters are messages, information and communications.

12/9/09 - 3:15 a.m.

I'm somewhere unfamiliar, struggling with a task I must learn to do. It's a personal chore and no one can help me. However, a kind friend or advisor speaks to me encouragingly as I struggle. There are thick semi-elastic bands that I must pull off my head and then pull back on again. They're tight and painful to remove and replace but I must continue doing this. My situation is frustrating, tedious and often discouraging. Whenever I succeed in twisting off one of the restricting bonds, I'm elated. At these times I'm cheered on by the unseen watcher nearby.

There are several rambunctious, excited youngsters around me who are creating miracles with little lights or flames that flare up but don't burn. These children belong to a new family here who are able to do these things. They're fascinating people and occasionally I get a few moments to interact with these truly unusual children. I understand that they cannot stay here long and wish I could be more free to be able to join them. But I'm obligated to keep on with my task of releasing and replacing these constrictive bands on my head. Maybe they loosen each time I stretch them over my head. Whether or not I understand, there's no choice; I must keep struggling with these restrictive bonds.

I woke from this dream with a sinus headache which throbbed painfully as I recorded the events. This was an example of how the physical body can influence a dream! Headaches and sinus issues have plagued me most of my adult life. These "small flames that don't

114

burn" were spiritual energies. They appeared in another dream which was previously published.

12/12/09 - 7:00 a.m.

Adventuring in a far-distant place, I'm on a trip with two busloads of people. We're in bathing suits, walking on coal-like ancient rocky terrain. The rough stones are grayish, not black. There's an ocean close by and, during the early part of our trek, we walk through shallow water near the shore. At the end of the dream, however, the tide has gone so far out that I can barely see the water. From time to time I pick up a few small pieces of rock that catch my attention. One stone in particular is fascinating; it's a light greenish-gray color, rolled smooth by the waves and has little weight. The stone is somewhat round and fits perfectly into the palm of my hand. It has an interesting texture with tiny grains of fine grit which feels like pumice. I decide to keep it as a souvenir.

Later, in a slightly different location and in shallow water, I pull up two items from a muddy area. They're pottery objects made, painted and intricately decorated by people in a long ago civilization. We have special guides here who are exceptionally knowledgeable about these artifacts and they give mini-lectures from time to time. The two pottery pieces I picked up are taken from me. The guides explain that no one is allowed to take any artifacts from this region. I think I end up without my piece of lava rock—unless I stuck it into a pocket of my bathing suit.

Now with the tide miles out and these uncomfortable rocks to walk over, I'm concerned about how long it will take to get home. A male nearby says, "We can leave the back way." We climb up a mud bank or sand dune, go through a rustic old building and then come out onto a sidewalk where the buses will pick us up!

I woke then, wondering what had happened to the lava rock. We were in the remains of an ancient civilization, perhaps in a very remote area on Earth. Our guides were of the spiritual variety and knew the history well. This ending seemed almost comedic!

3/12/10

I'm sleeping in my childhood bed and have just rolled over or shifted my position. Still mostly asleep, I'm startled when I feel something strange; the shifting movement is continuing beside my legs. Someone or something is most definitely here with me! I know this for certain and begin questioning, *insisting* to know who's here and what's going on. Finally, a male energy reluctantly acknowledges his presence and admits that he's been with me for many, many years. After a lengthy telepathic conversation he allows me to see him. He appears as a thin, slightly luminous yellow-white outline lying at the edge of the bed with his head on my pillow. He's very much at home here, relaxed and perfectly comfortable as though he belongs here—which apparently he does. This is a lot for me to comprehend! His lively conversation continues as he now moves around the room in his etheric form. This is an

extraordinary phenomenon which evidently will be an ongoing situation.

This was a fascinating dream and I actually *saw* this entity who confirmed that he'd been a presence in my life for a long time. Is he a guide or a nighttime protector? *Are* there such things? This was one of the strangest situations I've encountered in a dream.

7/15/10 - 3:30 a.m.
There's a bridge that I need to cross on the way to my destination. Partway across this bridge I have to stop because another car has had an accident and been abandoned here. The rest of the bridge is closed. I have to carefully back off the bridge and turn around.

Now I'm sitting on a table and a nurse is examining me. I question her about the accident—who was involved, is anyone hurt? She doesn't tell me anything. At this point, I believe I've reached my goal by another route but I don't understand why I'm being examined. I've already taken some of my belongings to other people. I had a definite purpose to give these things away, a 'mission of good will.'

A bridge symbolizes a transition between one place and another. I don't know if this accident is a touch of precognition but it appears that I'm tended to although unaware that I need attention. In the missing time segment I manage to partially get something done. Sharing belongings, such as the personal information in my books and implanted knowledge is, in fact, my mission in this lifetime as I understand it.

7/26/10 - 5:00 a.m.
I'm in a strange, plaster-like structure which is partially underground. It contains many oddly shaped rooms without doors, crude but serviceable. This is a temporary place where many people are crammed together in small personal areas with barely space for a bed and a place to hang a few clothes. These rooms nearly run together. The individual spaces and the short, curving walls between them have been decorated with colorful paints which help in finding one's way through this structural maze. There are no straight lines at all. The walls are curved and lumpy and join a low ceiling which is also lumpy and rounded. Everything is constructed entirely of this white plaster-like substance.

Now I'm in the outside area here. It may be evening or dusk when I go out but I have a feeling that it's always dim like this. There's a narrow street or sidewalk but no vehicles and very few people are outside. This white labyrinthine structure has been nicknamed "The Catacombs".

This underground dwelling was a very *real* place although I had no feeling about whether I was in the present, past or even a future time. This dream memory could have taken place on another planet; one without a bright sun.

8/25/10 - 4:00 a.m.
I'm sleeping in my bed when I become aware of the

118

presence of a husband/friend who has just entered the room. (He's no one I know in this life, but instantly I recognize him within the dream). **He communicates with me** (telepathically) **in a way that seems like soft speaking. As I begin to wake a little, my awareness shifts but I remain in this semi-sleep state as he lies down beside me. I listen to what he imparts directly into my mind. We are attuned mentally on the same wavelength although I'm in a slightly different reality. It's a very peaceful interlude. The images are clear and in full color. He does most of the 'talking' although I comment from time to time. Other than the initial shift I experienced to readjust my mental energy, this is completely effortless.**

(If you're not musical or have no piano handy, this example may mean nothing; however, it's a good illustration for those who understand music.) Musically speaking, this could be likened to playing a C major chord (CEGC) on a piano and then adding the 7th tone by moving the top note down a step to Bb. (CEGBb) This new chord causes the ear (energies) to want and *need to shift* to an F major chord (FCFA) for resolution.

Whatever this experience, it is extraordinarily peaceful and loving. I suspect this is my Unseen Companion or my Star Guardian and that I am given information which I've retained subconsciously. This dream is an excellent example of how mental telepathy works.

10/22/10 - 2:45 a.m.
Outdoors, while I'm walking with other people in a large circular formation, something amazing happens. We suddenly discover that we're able to do

119

fantastic things we never expected we could do. It's exhilarating! Then, one by one, these added enhancements begin to dissipate and finally disappear altogether.

There was so much *more* to this dream! I partially woke, mentally reviewing the incident and wishing that I could retain the special abilities I'd been given. Even though I'm still human, I would like to have kept my body structure as it is, *with* the enhancements.

I don't know what this dream was about nor did I even remember writing it on the page! There were wayward pencil marks on the paper, telltale indications that I had drifted off into sleep several times while trying to record the dream in the wee hours of the morning. I woke again at 4:50 a.m. with the pencil still clutched in my hand.

3/31/11 - 5:00 a.m.
I'm enjoying some kind of high-tech musical innovation! There's an interactive music staff on the wall that I'm watching as I listen to its beautiful chordal tones. When I touch a pencil point to a line or space on a smaller staff on the table in front of me, that note plays itself into the chord resounding overhead. It produces a gorgeous resonant, almost mesmerizing effect which sounds like a combination of harp, xylophone and marimba. It's nearly indescribable and the energy it produces makes my heart feel as though it's spinning! This will be waiting for me at school and I am anxious to get there.

I felt elated when I woke with this memory!

120

Music, especially pleasant-sounding, is a positive symbol. I've been involved with music all my life, so in this case it may be the addition of a novel twist to a familiar pursuit that has enraptured me. School indicates further education which is exciting for me within the context of this dream.

7/8/11 - 4:15 a.m.
There are some negative traits and useless habits which I've had for a long time. A voice is urging me to forcefully eject these things from my being. I'm pulling them out of me, throwing them down and stomping on them as hard as I can. Some are fairly easy to get out but others present a difficult struggle. The surroundings are clear and bright wherever I am. At times I can almost visualize the form of the Being who is vigorously advising me to rid myself of these unwanted parts. I sense it's a male energy, perhaps because of the power exuding from him as I obey without question or hesitation.

There were other segments of this dream that I couldn't recall after I rolled over to pick up my clipboard to write. They weren't as strong or meaningful as this section, which left me with a mild emotional exhaustion upon waking and remembering. This dream was similar to a couple of other cleansing, purging dreams I had years ago and included in my previous book.

8/2/11 - 4:30 a.m. Two separate but similar dreams came during the night:

#1. I'm engaged in a deep discussion with a man. It's a pleasant but very serious conversation. He's a guide/teacher/advisor figure and I'm a conscientious and dedicated student.

#2. This is a similar discussion, a bit lighter in tone, with a woman in the same capacity as the man. I am the serious student assigned to fulfill a mission, obligation or duty.

These dreams occurred at different times during the very early morning hours. I couldn't recall what I was told but both discussions were meaningful and important. The information has been embedded in my subconscious mind. Because the two dreams were so similar and both clearly recalled, they were intended to come to the attention of my conscious mind, simply to be aware that I've been advised or informed.

1/28/12 - 4:00 a.m.
The setting of this dream seems familiar; I've been here before. I'm outdoors on a bright, warm day at either a college campus or the grassy area in front of a cathedral-like church. A small group of eight or nine other people is here with me. There are silver keys which allow certain people access to something when we get inside this large building. It's an auspicious, important place and I'm holding one of these keys in my right hand.

There are also two sets of small index cards which contain short lines of writing or typing. On one set are rhyming lines. The other cards are different but

I can't recall what's on them. Previously I've seen both sets of cards but remember only this much about them. We, who are eligible to be given these cards, have also earned the privilege of receiving one of the silver keys. I'm prepared to mount the steps and enter the stately edifice to use my key for the first time. It's an awesome feeling.

Awesome was a perfect description for my emotion when I awoke with this dream. Even though other portions were not recalled, I was grateful for the pieces I did remember. It seems that something remarkable is pending in the near future. Keys unlock things, symbolizing opportunity and/or freedom. (In May I would discover that the odd dreams were actually memories.)

2/10/12 - 4:50 a.m.
The scene is an operatory similar to a medical or dental office. Someone has just put a couple of stickers on me! I sense his presence but cannot see him. These stickers are oval-shaped shiny paper or plastic, medium pea-green colored and they have a short word printed on them in black letters.

I know that I saw and read the word and I'm almost positive it said STAR. This is what came to mind when I tried to remember what I'd seen. Now after pondering it, star would be perfectly appropriate, which is probably why I'm second-guessing myself. I believe that this presence or energy was my Star Guardian.

I sent this special dream to Diane Tessman, who, in 1983, was the first to identify me as a "Star Person." Here is her response:

"As you know, dreams of importance sometimes have 'markers' or a symbol given during the dream. I had one with my 'Guardian', where he was wearing an Australian-
type hat, the kind with baubles hanging off
like you are going into the outback. It was
teal blue of all things and had no baubles.
But I thought, 'What the heck?' The dream
was otherwise significant and meaningful
and I then realized that the hat was the
'marker' of that dream, simply put there to
make me remember it. And it sounds like
the sticker with 'star' was a marker in your
dream."

9/15/12 - 5:15 a.m.
**I'm hovering over an unfamiliar scene, intently
watching something below. There's someone with
me—so familiar that he's like another part of myself. At first I can't discern whether he's explaining a
situation to me or whether I'm learning to watch,
interpret and explain it to him. All conversation is
telepathic.**

**Below us is a dilapidated old shed in a dried-up fal-
low or abandoned crop field. Inside the shed are two
dark-skinned men between 30 and 45 years old. One
is seated awkwardly on the dusty floor. The other is
leaning forward, imploring him to do something.
Evidently my Unseen Companion prompts me to focus more intently to determine the situation, because
now I extend a keener perception into the scene. I
understand that there's something wrong with the**

seated man. He's mentally and physically disabled, lacking in brain and body the normal attributes of a human being. The other man is related to him and has been sent to find and bring him home. There's a feeling of caring but this other man must use power in a somewhat negative way to accomplish his assignment. I relay this information to my Teacher and we have a short telepathic conversation, (none of which I recall.) Now, the messenger has pulled the other man to his feet and they're outside the shed. The disabled one is staggering along in an awkward, ungainly way as he attempts to hurry ahead of the other man. He's thin, tall and lanky, wearing ill-fitting trousers and an old plaid shirt. I sense—but do not actually see—that he is barefoot.

This was a teaching dream experience in another dimension and time. All was very clear, quiet and intensely focused. My Unseen Companion was behind and to my right side, where he usually is. I felt somewhat like a periscope as I learned to 'extend my perception' and I keenly felt the intense emotions of this relationship and situation below.

3/1/13 - 5:12 a.m.
I'm looking across a wide hallway into a large room on the other side of this unfamiliar house. There's a huge window on the far wall which may encompass the entire side of that room. It's so clear that it seems there's no glass at all. There are people in that room whom I don't see although we've been conversing telepathically. The room I'm in is a bedroom and it's understood that I must stay here. I'm not

allowed to go across the hall where the others are . . . not yet, anyway. This is not a punishment; it's a rule that I accept unquestioningly.

Now something unusual is happening beyond that far window. I'm seeing the gentle movement of what appear to be large fluffy feathers floating down from the sky. A beautiful pink glow from either the sky or the feathers themselves is making them appear iridescent and sparkling. I glance over to my right at the small picture window in my room. Huge white, puffy flakes which I instantly recognize as snow are wafting down against a backdrop of light gray sky. I look again at the far window. Glistening pink feathery snow is still drifting down there. I call out excitedly to the people in that room, "Look at that beautiful snow!" I'm entranced by this magical moment.

Symbolically, hallways signify change; literally, a pathway across or to somewhere else. There are spiritual Beings in the room across this hallway. I'm not ready to "cross over to the other side" yet—although I'm able to appreciate some of it from a distance. Pink represents unconditional love. The clarity in dreams is usually 20/20. I sense that this dream scenario was a little gift from Spirit. (At this time I was still listless from the effects of the flu—and my hair was falling out.)

8/22/13 - 4:00 a.m.
There's a woman with me whom I never see. We've been working together somewhere . . . maybe in space because I see nothing at all and have a sense of

vast openness. I become aware of this when there's a problem; we're being interfered with or interrupted. The woman suggests that we go to another location. Immediately we're moving—gliding or flying smoothly through space together. The sensation is like riding in an open car—without a car. We arrive at her home area; the house is over to the right but we stay outdoors. I settle myself on top of a picnic table. A little girl comes running over with the woman's husband just behind her. The woman tells her child that she's busy and to be good. The husband understands what needs to be done.

A partial wall now appears on the far side of this table. The man takes the cord that's attached to a lightweight frame or cap which is on my head and plugs the small narrow end of it into a socket in the wall. Evidently this little device has been on my head the entire time. The headgear is now reactivated and the programming will be completed. It's the transfer of information to my mind via this woven brown cap. My hair appears to be brown also. I feel no discomfort and understand that this is part of my training. The procedure is vaguely familiar to me. Nothing seems strange except having to come here to the woman's home due to an unexpected disturbance.

The disturbance turned out to be one of my cats nudging me to wake up! I was glad to remember the dream and immediately wrote it down. It revealed a more technical way than telepathy to impart knowledge to a human mind. Brown hair shows my dream self to be considerably younger than my physical self!

That evening my Guided Writing commented:

"This morning's dream was especially good for the book in symbolic form but very true as to how you are being given information which is implanted—if you choose to use that word in this way—into your subconscious mind for retrieval at the time when you are tuned to a higher vibration." (Notice that this information came in one very long sentence. They give the information; the human must put it into words and add the punctuation.)

8/27/13 - 2:30 a.m.

The scene is unfamiliar but clear, bright and very *real* in some indescribable way. There's a man here who is very ill. He's about 40 years old and thin now, emaciated from his ailment. I love this man deeply. At one time he was an excellent, perhaps famous tennis player but is now out of the public eye and staying at a private place. There's a large swimming pool here just outside our room. At times, I seem to be watching all this as though a movie is being made; however, my emotions are much too strongly involved for this to be playacting. The situation is absolutely real. I lie down beside him on our bed and hug him gently. I try to *will* my strength and health into his frail body and weep quietly, not wanting him to be aware of my utter pathos.

Now we're in the swimming pool. Again I have the sense that this is being filmed; that I'm literally "in

128

**the scene" living it in reality at the same moment
that I'm also observing it from a slightly separate
part of myself. I stay at this man's side supporting
him physically, mentally and emotionally with every
part of my being. It's a tragic situation. I know this
man so well, love him deeply and know that his condition is terminal.**

After recording and studying this dream, I wonder if somehow I have apprehended the circumstances
and personal emotions of another woman somewhere.
This *has* to have been a real situation, yet it has no rele-
vance to my present waking life. Is it possible that this
is a life in another dimension which has bled through to
the dimension where my astral body was during the
night?

That evening the Guided Writing had a very brief
comment:

> *"Your dream? Yes, a very loving marriage
> in another dimension playing itself out."*

In contrast to the long, explanatory sentence after the
previous dream, this one was ultra brief and I missed
the point of how *I* was involved.

12/11/13 - 3:45 a.m.
**I'm a female military nurse or medic in a foreign
post caring for young post-surgical soldiers. They're
heavily medicated when I'm first assigned to them.
All of these young men will survive their physical
traumas but their minds are the real problem. My
job is to calm these men and soothe their trauma-**

tized psychological states as they gradually become conscious. It's a very emotionally draining situation for them and for me too. There are other young women here doing this work with me. For a moment I hover briefly above the small area where we sleep and stay until we're called out to attend another post-op patient. I note that my hair is short and medium-dark colored and I'm wearing white or light-colored clothing.

Now I approach the bed of my next patient. We're in a large and somewhat open building with many beds but I look only at the young soldier I'm here to attend. He's delirious, talking to himself or anyone he senses around him; he's frightened and confused. I speak gently, calling him by name and doing what I can to soothe and reassure him that he's going to be okay now. In a nearby outdoor area I see young men getting out of a vehicle and being wrestled into restraints and straight jackets. They appear physically undamaged except for their minds. It's stressful for me to observe this and is obviously upsetting to those GIs as well as for the other soldiers and medics who have to subdue them this way.

The final scene is a small, quiet chapel situated at the end of a hallway in the large building. I stand at the back of the area where a religious service is in progress for the 30 or so people seated inside. One of my patients suddenly appears behind us in the doorway. He has gotten out of his bed and been searching for me. The service is momentarily disrupted. I walk him back to his bed and will stay and

calm him down for a while. He has bonded with me, for I represent security—a link to home and normal life. As I begin to wake, I feel sad and depressed, wondering why it is we have to have wars.

I've been told many times by my Guidance that I have dreams I don't remember. This emotional one shows how my waking life could be influenced in a negative way by clearly recalling many dreams of this sort. I know this one is very *real*, which makes it even heavier on my heart.

My Guided Writing that evening had a few comments:

> *"We are here. You think of your dream this morning and wonder if it was real—were you attending wounded GIs during your sleep? Your answer is yes. You do healing work and have been so doing for a great many years. There is much involved in your mission both awake and in other dimensions. Did you sense anyone with you—a guide or companion? No, you did not. There are many tasks you do by yourself; you do not always need a guide or teacher for things you have learned to do on your own. Yes, you saw yourself young and with dark hair. You can choose your 'garment' when in the astral state. When working with youthful people it is fitting to look like them. This is a good dream to include in your book; perhaps the final dream."*

And so it shall be the final dream in this section of Special Dreams.

"Knowledge advances by steps not leaps."

- Thomas B. Macaulay
English Historian, Essayist, Statesman
(1800-1859)

CHAPTER FIVE

Anomalies:

Visualizations
Experiences
The Final Messages

VISUALIZATIONS

A visualization is a mental image, picture or impression which appears spontaneously. These images can appear at any time, most frequently on the verge of sleep or, after sleeping, just as you begin to wake. The following visualizations are not related in any way to my everyday life. I find these images quite interesting and, except for one which I requested, I have no explanation for why they appear, where they come from or, usually, what they mean.

6/7/11 - 5:28 a.m.
While I'm dozing, the word *Chalade* pops into my mind. I see it clearly just for a second and immediately know it's a French word and pronounced *shah lahd*. This is confirmed later when I look it up on the internet.

La Chalade is the name of a Cistercian abbey founded on June 6, 1128. The abbey closed in 1790 and is now an historical monument in Meuse, France. The Cistercians, named after the village of Citeaux, near Dijon, is a Catholic religious order of enclosed monks and nuns. They are also known as Bernardines or White Monks, referring to the white habit covered by a black scapular, a long, sleeveless, belted vest open at the sides.

As I typed the information for this book, I noticed that the dates of the founding of La Chalade and this visualization are *within a day of each other*, minus 883 years. Was this *coincidental?*

La Chalade

6/24/11 - 3:00 a.m.
A young man in a very pale cream-colored suit or outfit walks out into space and begins a slow, graceful dance as though on stage. He is surrounded by illumination, about 20 feet from me and slightly elevated above my eye level. His figure is amazingly lithe and exudes an aura of elegance. There is nothing else in view and after ten seconds the clear visualization disappears.

Like some visualizations, this one gave no indication of what it represents. The figure could be a guide, an angel or simply a spiritual energy who happened by and put on a brief performance for me.

7/15/11
During the start of my evening meditation, a dim gray and white vision appears to the right of center in my mind's eye. It's a powerful gray-robed

138

male figure. His right foot, closer to me, is on the ground; his left foot is propped up slightly on something, perhaps a rock or a low step. The cloak and hood obscure his face. His left arm is about waist-high and in that hand he holds a tall, straight walking stick or staff. He may be slightly resting on this staff because I have the impression that the other end is firmly planted on the ground.

There was no message; only the sense that he is a powerful figure. He may be a guide who simply chose to be seen at this particular time.

7/30/11 - 3:00 a.m.
I see a flash of bright, vivid colors and then a tiny flying female being appears and hovers near me. She is a miniature humanoid with two arms and legs, a human head and face. Her hair is very dark and close-cropped and comes to points at the center of her forehead and in front of her ears. Her remarkable eyes catch my attention; they're diamond-shaped with dark lids. Two sets of small, delicate wings flutter on her upper back or shoulders in a manner similar to a dragonfly's wing movement. As soon as I take in these details, she vanishes.

Some people might consider this little creature a fairy. Whatever she was, she was fascinating!

2/8/12 - 9:00 a.m.
There is a huge, dark brown round-shaped rock with an opening . . . it's a cave entrance. I'm hover-

ing in the air in front of and slightly to the left of this scene. A robed figure emerges from inside the dimly lit entrance, then stands still, looking outward. From slightly behind my line of vision on the right comes another robed figure, followed closely by one more. They approach the cave entrance and glide in past the original figure. (I have some difficulty holding the image because my eyelids are twitching with the effort to see more intently.)

The rock cave entrance is clear again and once more the same robed figure steps to the opening. This time he holds a green neon-like flame. It has a fairly steady glow which is not flickering, yet seems 'alive' in some way. Now a shorter figure, also wearing a robe, approaches the cave entrance from my right, moving slowly as if somewhat unsure of him—or herself. This figure particularly draws my attention and also a tug of emotion. Then it decisively hurries on into the cave. (Again there is interference with my eyelids twitching.)

Now I see sliding panels of rock emerging slowly from each side of the cave entrance. They meet in the center and seal the entrance so that it now looks like a solid rock.

The color of this illuminated torch was the 'growing green' of leaves in early spring. Dreaming of or seeing a cave suggests that a transformation or rebirth may come about. Robed figures are indications of spiritual Beings. There was a positive feeling as the scene ended.

140

3/19/12 - 3:55 p.m.

The image of a bald eagle appears behind my closed eyes. It's very close to me and I see only its face and a bit of white cloud far behind it. The eagle stares intensely at me. White and light gray feathers cover its head. At first the eyes are dark but suddenly they light up and become exceptionally bright with a piercing whiteness! This brilliance radiates, scintillating outward like many tiny spokes.

This image lasted about ten full seconds as I focused specifically on those eyes to be certain of what I was seeing. This was an awesome visualization. Eagles can represent courage and perceptiveness and, to me, ferocity.

4/20/12 - 9:30 p.m.

As I glide along a wooded pathway I notice a bright greenish-yellow glow coming from something just ahead on my left. I stop there and gaze incredulously at a strange little creature sitting in the opening of a small, hollowed-out gourd or squash-like vegetable. It's a tiny, pale humanoid staring directly at me. Its head is totally bald and has a bony, almost skeletal look. The glow appears to be emanating like an aura all around this little figure. It doesn't move but I sense that it is definitely sentient and somewhat startled. I stay perfectly still and simply stare back until the visualization disappears.

My discovery of this other-dimensional creature's home startled us both. These beings are called devas (day-vahz)—a Sanskrit word meaning "being of brilliant light." Devas are nature spirits, elementals and fairies. They're composed of non-physical *astral* energies and, although humanoid in appearance, they are not human.

4/23/12 - 2:00 p.m.
While resting after lunch, an image in sepia tones comes clearly into view behind my closed eyes. It's a large owl with 'horns' and speckled feathers perched on a thick, gnarled branch. Behind the owl is a beautiful full moon. A feeling of peacefulness pervades this visualization.

I have mixed emotions about owls. After my great-grandmother passed on, our family visited my grandparents and I slept in Grammy's room. Just outside the only window was a tall pine tree where a small light brown owl perched nearly every night and hooted softly. At first it frightened me because I'd never seen or heard a real owl before and this one was very close. Cautiously, I got out of bed on the second night just to watch and listen to it. My presence didn't appear to bother it and I'm sure it was aware of me there. What disturbs me about owls is their intense, large-eyed *stare* which seems invasive and makes me feel uneasy.

4/27/12 - 1:30 p.m.
Dozing after lunch I see the owl again! This time it's on the right side of my visual field with its back turned toward me. The back of its head and upper body, which are all I see, are speckled as before. However, the backs of the feathery tufts atop its head are very dark colored and I understand that's

what I'm to notice.

I recorded this surprising and curious second look at the owl, then sketched the back of its head and colored in the tufts. It was an odd little incident coming four days after the first visualization. Owls symbolize wisdom and intuition. It's also been said that owls have been used by ETs as a screen image to block out any conscious memory of experiences with them.

I sent descriptions of these visualizations to a friend who responded with this comment: "It's a bet that you're being monitored closely." When he read my first book, this friend realized that I had been abducted but he didn't mention this until after I came to the realization myself and wrote to him.

8/17/12 - 5:00 a.m.
I'm finally falling back to sleep after a restless night when I'm startled by an unusual scene that suddenly appears behind my closed eyelids. I'm peering through a narrow horizontal window at a life-sized photograph of a group of men. The image of one of these men is more prominent and lifelike, as though he's singled out from the rest. I understand that this is not a current image of him—in reality he is older than he appears to me at this moment. He's a nice-looking man without facial hair and a relatively slim, muscular build and is wearing a military uniform with a black beret. I sense that he's from a foreign country, possibly a leader or in an important position. Behind and above him is a plain light yellow wall.

Suddenly there is movement: a long, very narrow panel appears across the entire scene at the level of this man's head. The left edge of the panel turns black and instantly, like a line of black ink, it flows rapidly across to the right. As it passes through the man's head, his entire image disappears from view. The moment the black color reaches the far right side, the panel and photograph are gone. There is nothing left to see but the blank pale yellow wall. Then the entire visualization disappears.

There was no accompanying emotion with this visualization; in fact, it was like being in a total void. I feel that that this visualization could turn out to be pre-cognitive.

9/29/12 - 8:30 p.m.
As I settled down for my prayer and meditation time, I asked to see my Star Guardian, if that would be possible—or even just a sign to know that he heard my request. As I began to slow and deepen my breathing to relax, a bright, 'living' blue and white light flashed into view behind my left eye/forehead area and I felt a quickening in my chest or heart.

This light had a definite three-dimensional shape which was somewhat circular, yet with soft angles. It was a rich cobalt/royal blue color, shining and *alive* with streaks of blazing white within and around it. The image lasted only about two seconds and the accompanying sudden emotional quiver made me believe that my request was heard.

10/29/12 - 3:00 a.m.
I'm standing in the witness box of a small courtroom somewhere. There is a great deal of tension in the room. While the other people here are involved in a discussion at the far side of the room, I write myself a note on the worn, smooth wooden railing in front of me. Holding a pen in my left hand, I write, "How did he know about the money?" I want to be sure to ask this vital question when I'm interrogated. Curiously, I notice that this doesn't look like my handwriting, even though I'm left-handed. The preliminary hearing concerns something quite worrisome and very serious, involving espionage, double-dealing and weapons.

I feel that I've been superimposed over someone else in this visualization and that the focus concerns the current situation in Ben Ghazi where our U.S. Ambassador and three other men were murdered in an attack on the embassy. Whether this is a future courtroom situation, I don't know, but this intense moment definitely has a precognitive feel to it.

5/25/13 - 3:00 p.m.
Resting on my bed, I'm nearly asleep when suddenly behind my closed eyes, the close-up face of a man appears. He has long fluffy white hair, a white moustache, beard and bushy white eyebrows. At first his pale blue eyes seem to be sparkling but then a brilliantly clear light beams outward from them. These lights radiate upward even as he continues to look directly at me. After several seconds the image is gone.

145

This was one of the most startling things I've ever visualized, probably because it appeared right in front of my face! I don't know who he was or why he chose to stare at me like this but it had a powerful effect when his eyes flashed out so brightly!

Visualizations are unpredictable and inexplicable —unless you've asked for one, which I do from time to time on a whim. But then I might ask, from whence comes the whim?

EXPERIENCES

This final section is not about dreams at all, although in a few instances the semi-conscious events were precipitated by dreams. Most of these anomalies simply came "out of nowhere."

In late 1978 or early 1979 I took a six-week meditation class at the local community college on Cape Cod. My guides and the Guided Writing had been urging me to meditate but it was frustrating because my mind just wouldn't stay still! Each week the instructor taught us a different type of meditation. At home one afternoon I worked very hard to get into the particular state-of-mind and I actually *did* reach or contact something. The feeling, or whatever it was, touched me so deeply that I burst into tears and sobbed helplessly for a long while. I felt desperately *homesick* for some thing or place that I couldn't identify. Possibly I made a momentary contact with the energy of a familiar place in a spiritual dimension. Since then my efforts at meditation have never been much more than frustration. During my sleep I contact these realms much more easily. My present evening meditation period is simply softly spoken prayer, one-sided conversation with my guidance and sending love and healing energy to family, friends and others.

7/16/89
At some point toward morning I hear and feel a snapping sound somewhere in my upper body which instantly wakes me. I understand that something has been released.

147

What could possibly 'snap' around the chest/neck area? This little message-like anomaly could be symbolic; about this time a long, drawn-out divorce issue finally had been settled. Otherwise, I really don't know what to think about this strange experience.

8/18/09 - 1:30 a.m.

Something wakes me during a very restless night. When I open my eyes, I see that the entire area behind my closed thermal and light-blocking drapery is lit up extremely brightly for a full three to five seconds. I strain to hear the sound of anything unusual. All is silent. I glance at the clock; it's 1:30 in the morning. Nothing—not sunlight or car headlights—could possibly penetrate this thermal drapery, yet *something* did! I wake easily and my hearing is excellent. I'm positive that I was conscious when I saw an incredibly bright light beam *through* the thick drapes which cover the French doors of my second floor bedroom at the front of the house.

4/6/11

In the early morning I begin to wake with the memory of being buried in mud! There are many of us here and we're all very confused. Everything happened so fast that we were totally helpless; we couldn't save ourselves.

I realize that I must have been dreaming and I lie here a moment to collect my thoughts and record it. But a stronger—or telepathic—thought comes to mind and I understand that "This really happened . . . there *was* an earthquake and flood." My conscious mind takes over and determines that I wasn't dreaming; I was simply

148

remembering about the earthquake and tsunami that hit part of Japan a couple of weeks ago. I rationalize that this really didn't happen to me and I go back to sleep.

Now at 6:00 a.m. I know that I was actually hovering among the confused mental energies of other souls. I suspect that the last horrific memories of the people who were drowned are 'stuck in astral essence' and hovering around the area where their bodies are buried in the mud. Their souls have gone on into the spiritual dimensions but their *emotional memories* linger in the denser planetary energy. I believe that my astral form was there among these energies, maybe trying to free them in some way. In fact, I may have returned there to help after falling back to sleep earlier because I felt very dizzy as I got out of bed shortly after 6:00. I had to steady myself on the walls and doorways until my internal balance adjusted itself. This was an exceptionally realistic experience!

Nov. or Dec. 2011 - 8:00 or 8:30 p.m.

I never thought to record this incident at the time but remember it clearly.

I was upstairs in my bedroom which is located at the front of the house. Suddenly there were several tremendously loud knocks on the front door, so forceful that the crystals on the upstairs French door tapped sharply against the glass! It startled me and sent the cats scurrying under the bed. My first thought was that someone strong and extremely angry was trying to break in. I was running downstairs to tell my husband, when the thunderous knocking came again in precisely measured beats. As I reached Eric's room, I heard three more resounding knocks. I asked Eric if he could hear them; he could, but thought the noise was probably mortar drills from the army base. After that third series there was silence. I went back upstairs, now listening intently for the sound of a car engine or footsteps on the driveway. There was nothing, nor any indication that the military base was holding drills.

On March 22, 2012, I asked Eric if he remembered the loud pounding on the front door. He did but said again that it must have been from the army base. I asked if he recalled approximately when that happened and he replied, "About three months ago." Two years after the incident, I searched the internet and found that other people also had experiences with what is called the "Nine Knocks Phenomenon"—three sequences of three loud knocks from no apparent cause or source.

5/28/12

While meditating shortly after 9 p.m., I noticed the distinctive and familiar scent of witch hazel. This was the first time I had smelled it in many years. My father always splashed it on his face after shaving. The scent and memory brought an instant tug of emotion and I mentally sent out a "Hi, Dad!" message.

9/22/12 - 5:00 a.m.

In a semi-doze or light sleeping state, I'm suddenly aware of a rapid triplicate rhythm gently tapping inside my head. It's a delicate physical pulsation in a fast waltz tempo. As I focus my attention on it I become more consciously awake.

This unusual sensation was similar to one that I'd

experienced before and ignored. This time I reached for my wrist to be sure it wasn't an irregular pulse. It was not, so I simply recorded the anomaly.

9/30/12

At about 5:30 in the morning I'm startled by a quasi-physical sensation at my chest, more to the left side than centered. It was a fairly rapid pulsation which ran diagonally from my left shoulder joint to almost the center of my chest. It wasn't *in* my chest but more just under the skin, almost on the surface. It pulsed back and forth for at least a full minute and then stopped.

At first this strange fluttering startled me but I sensed that it was something purposeful and not a physical problem. I wondered if it was a 'tune-up' of some sort because I could almost visualize the instrument making this trilling vibration—a narrow rod with tiny rounded knobs on either end. No further thought came to mind, so this remains another inexplicable experience.

3/13/13 - 8:45 p.m.

I was driving home from a Wednesday night choir rehearsal.The weather was clear and there wasn't much traffic on U.S. #1 as I moved along at 55 mph, the posted speed limit. I happened to glance up at the sky and noticed two very bright white lights, side by side with a space between them. They were not moving and were much too big and bright to be stars. I sensed that they were attached to something but I didn't see anything behind them. Slowing the car, I kept watching as closely as I could. The two lights were solitary in the dark sky and remained absolutely stationary. I didn't notice any stars although I wasn't looking for anything else at the time.

Then I thought, "Oh, wow! This might be a UFO!" Immediately a mild electrical tingling went through me from my chest into my spine. I *knew* this was confirmation that it *was* a UFO! I wanted to stop the car and get out to just watch it for a while but for safety's sake I kept driving slowly and watching as best I could. When I came to a stand of tall pine trees which blocked my view, I wasn't able to see the lights anymore. I got into the left turn lane, drove down the hill and went home where too many trees obscured my view of the sky.

A week later the Guided Writing of 3/20/13 said:

> *"We are here. Yes, you saw one of our craft in your sky last week. We confirmed with a signal and you felt it. Of course we knew where you were; we wanted you to see us. We love you and are protecting you from harm. You may see us again."*

This incident reminds me of a short discussion about a year ago in the adult Bible study class. There were seven of us present that Sunday and I asked if anyone had seen a UFO. Four of the seven members present raised their hands. I wasn't one of them but I recall thinking how amazing it was that more than half of this group had actually seen a UFO!

5/21/13

I had been asleep for several hours when the doorbell rang. The chime box is on the wall at the bottom of the staircase and my bedroom door is left ajar at night so the cats can wander in and out. The doorbell has the familiar "ding-dong" tones and it chimes twice. I'm certain that the bell actually rang because both cats leaped off the bed and scrambled underneath it. I glanced at the clock; it was 1:14 a.m. I sat quietly on the bed, ears attuned for the sound of footsteps, a car door – anything. There was total silence. Tiptoeing quietly, I listened intently at the partially opened French door which faces the front of the house and is almost directly over the front door. There was no sound. As quietly as possible, I closed and locked that door and then hurried to the back of the house where the door to a second floor deck was partially open. I quietly closed and locked it, then sat on the top step of the staircase, still listening for any unusual sound. There was nothing and, after 20 minutes or so, I went back to bed.

When it was daylight I went outside through the garage to check the front door, doorstep and mat. Nothing unusual was there. What would cause a doorbell to ring in the middle of the night? I wondered if this might be another phenomenon like the 'Nine Knocks' and checked the internet. According to that source, doorbell ringing is not so unusual. Many people have experienced this and most believe it's caused by a glitch in the wiring—whether hard-wired or battery operated. Ours is the latter and was about six months to a year old at the time of this incident. It has never happened since. We changed the batteries in early November 2013 when the doorbell stopped working.

6/15/13 - 2:30 p.m.
During a nap, I heard a male voice clearly speak

my name. It wasn't loud, as if to get my attention, but more as though someone just happened to see me, knew who I was and said, "Oh, there's Joan . . ." except that only my name was audible. I heard it so clearly that I partially woke, wondering who had spoken. As I became more conscious I realized it must have been Eric. I tried to respond but could barely even hear myself attempt to say, "Yes?" Still unable to move, I lay still and "tuned in" to the tone of the voice. It really didn't sound like Eric yet it was familiar. After ten minutes I got up, went downstairs and asked my husband if he had called me. He had not.

Later I went for a 30-minute walk and again pondered that voice. An immediate thought came to mind that it might have been that of my first husband who died unexpectedly in August 2011. In that case, the voice would have been telepathic, which I would have heard clearly. Otherwise, I have no idea who it could have been.

That evening my Guided Writing commented:

> "*You* did *hear a voice speak your name today. Yes, someone you know, now in spirit. You will hear more in time.*"

In February, while I was re-reading all dreams for the final editing before the manuscript is sent to be published, a clear image from a well-known story flashed through my mind when I read this experience again. In *The Christmas Carol* by Charles Dickens, one of the three ghosts takes Scrooge and points out people from his early life and comments on what might have been. I believe that my first husband was having a similar "tour of the past" as part of a life review with his spiritual guardian.

7/27/13 - 2:00 a.m.
I was sleeping in a twin bed at a condominium at the shore. Just as I moved one of my feet, I heard two distinct meows inside my head. The first was Gabby's high, clear voice; the second was Angie's little 'burbling' voice! They had been lying at the foot of the bed in their astral forms! I had plugs in my ears to muffle the sound of the noisy air conditioner. The cats were *physically* sleeping at home but their *astral* bodies were sleeping on my bed here at the beach. Like humans, cats can send telepathic messages!

Angie and Gabby

FINAL MESSAGES

When I was finished writing *Journey of Dreams*, I got a little telepathic message during a meditation. I immediately wrote it down and decided to use it as a final message for the book.

> "The greatest blessing of all for human beings is that every night we get to go Home for a visit, whether or not we remember. These visits make our final transition a familiar, comforting and most welcoming Homecoming indeed!"

As I contemplated a final message for *Secret Contact*, I reread the last chapter of *Journey of Dreams*. Two of the dreams in the last chapter were symbolic. Now, three years later, I believe I have a better understanding of what those dreams mean. I've put their 'essence' together for a final message that is interesting to contemplate.

I believe that extraterrestrial aliens have been visiting this planet from the time it was stable enough to support life. There are many races of alien beings in and around the Earth at this time. At least one race of spiritual Entities has been in my life for over 70 years, guiding and teaching me during my sleep. I know that messages have been put into my subconscious mind while I sleep and I believe that at some point during my lifetime these will be released.

Across our planet are millions of other humans

who also have been contacted during sleep. The spiritually evolved ETs have been working with humanity from the inside! In 1971, when I first became aware that something strange was happening to me during the night, there were no support groups or books to turn to. Now there are many sources for help and understanding for those of us who, I believe, agreed to participate in a plan to help our civilization of humanity evolve. The truth has begun to emerge despite all efforts by government and media to keep it submerged.

I believe that subconscious memories which are stored in minds around the world will be triggered and released at some point in the not too distant future. I believe that all of humanity will simultaneously receive a telepathic message which will be understood in every language. Those who have been given individual messages during sleep will then be able to help the people in their communities who will be in shock and disbelief. The humans who are ready and able to move on to the next level of evolution will do so. Those who are confused, in crisis and chaos will be helped by the 'contactees', the 'go-betweens' and 'messengers' who will step forward to aid and assist those struggling with the new information.

To the best of my present ability to understand, this is what I believe may happen—unless a nuclear accident or disaster comes first and eliminates humanity altogether—again.

Epilogue

I'm a much different person now than I was in 2009 when I began to re-read over 2,000 dreams I had recorded so that I could write a book about them. Not that I wanted to write a book at all—I was *compelled* to do it . . . irresistibly urged by Beings who had been in my dreams and who had been guiding my thoughts onto paper for years. I was aware that my odd dreams were strange yet I included 41 of them in that first book, which was published in May 2011.

Four months later I was informed that I was to write *another* book! My Guidance didn't mention it again until the following March when They said to begin the next book where the first one left off. They told me to re-read all my old dreams again to discover what the theme or topic would be and that there would be new developments and revelations in my life. They said that this second book should be published in early 2014. I got busy marching to my new orders. In May of 2012 I bought an old paperback book about UFO abductions and discovered the incredible purpose for this second book.

National Geographic Channel conducted a survey in July 2012 that revealed that 36% of Americans polled believe that UFOs are real. That's 80 million people! Ten percent of those believe that they have seen a UFO and, interestingly, 79% of these Americans believe that the government is withholding information from us.

Now that *Secret Contact* is completed, my next step is clear; I need to write a final book about the rest of my story. That book will require a series of hypnotic regressions to delve into my subconscious mind for as much information as will be released. It's a normal part of human nature to be fearful of anything unfamiliar or strange but I need to do this, not only for my own edification but because it's the last part of my mission! All revelations of my encounters with extraterrestrial aliens these many years will be recorded. I will transcribe and publish the results and share them with you.

I sincerely hope that this present work has given encouragement to others who think they might have encountered extraterrestrial life forms. There are a great many of us on Earth now; we need to step forward and show support for each other. We truly are not alone.

Joan Bridgeman
April 2014

Acknowledgments

I first wish to thank my husband who, although he doesn't always go along with my beliefs, gives me the space to share them.

I acknowledge my sons, Greg and Robert, for staying in touch and accepting my idiosyncrasies.

I'm grateful to all the many musicians and singers who have helped me keep harmony and joy in my life throughout the years.

I acknowledge my friends near and far, seen and unseen.

I'm grateful for the array of fur-bearing, four-legged companions, which have graced my life with unconditional love.

I thank Karen Mireau, who appeared just when I needed an open-minded, creative person to publish this book.

And I thank and acknowledge those Beings in other dimensions who guide, teach and protect me and many other humans.

Glossary

Abduction – being taken to a UFO, examined and returned.

Astral – relating to the stars; ethereal energy; a less dense dimensional reality or plane.

Astral body – a likeness of the physical body composed of astral energy which releases itself from the physical during sleep or when unconscious.

Astral cord – a stretchy 'tunnel-like' etheric/ectoplasmic form that connects the astral body to the physical body during sleep. (It looks like an X-ray of the small intestine!) Also called 'the silver cord' in ancient religious texts.

Being – when capitalized, refers to an intelligent, spiritually evolved entity in or from another dimension.

Entity – an other-dimensional energy; any being from another reality.

ETs or Extraterrestrials – intelligent paraphysical beings who can appear in our three-dimensional world as well as their own multidimensional realities.

Etheric – vaporous, misty-appearing substance in the dimensional realm of dreams.

Exoterrestrials – extraterrestials. See 'ETs'.

Guardian – a Being who accompanies and protects us during sleep; observes and supports by his or her presence but does not engage in the activities of the dreams.

Greys – short, spindly humanoids with overly-large heads, huge dark eyes, tiny noses, lips and ear holes who possess powerful psychic energy; these androids have a 'hive' mentality and are devoid of emotions.

Group travel – feeling stuck within a strong energy with one or more other people, all moving together as though in a vehicle but without any vehicle.

Guides – spiritual entities who accompany us in dreams; often familiar energies, like friends or companions who support us in our endeavors.

Guided Writing – mental impressions sensed and transferred to paper. The Source described itself to me as *"Wide and great Beings who watch over many of you there. Some of us are close to just you; others of us are parts of yourself. We coordinate to send you information you need."*

Light Beings – white-robed etheric Beings, or bright orbs of white or colored light.

Out-of-body – the experience of becoming aware when in the astral body, that you are able to fly, glide and have perfect vision; also called astral projection.

Star Guardian – one specific, never seen Being who has an inter-dimensional link with some humans; he guides, protects and can take us to visit other places and planets. Not everyone is assigned a Star Guardian.

Star People – individual souls who have chosen, or been chosen, to take human incarnation and work with inter-dimensional Beings at this time in Earth's history.

Symbolism – the language of the subconscious; images that represent something, not the literal image that may appear in the dream. Example: water = emotions.

Teachers – Spiritual Beings who meet with us to educate our souls.

Telepathy – conversing through mental energies; sending and receiving mental impressions; this occurs naturally during sleep.

Time travel – the ability to visit the past or the future in other dimensions during sleep.

Transporters – small androids (collectively called Greys); paraphysical robotic beings with a hive mentality; programmed to transport a human astral form to a UFO; they can change their appearances (shape-shift).

UFOs – solid or semi-solid inter-dimensional space craft of various shapes and sizes.

Unseen Companion – the specific Being I recognize in my dreams by his strong energy just behind my right shoulder; he is also a Teacher, Guide and probably the same entity I call my Star Guardian.

Visualization – appearance of a spontaneous image behind closed eyes, often on the edges of sleep.

Bibliography

Books:

Brown, Courtney, Ph.D.
Cosmic Voyage
Onyx Penguin Group, New York, NY, 1996.
Cosmic Explorers
Signet Penguin Putnam, New York, NY, 1999.
www.courtneybrown.com

Cannon, Dolores
Keepers of the Garden
Ozark Mountain Publishing, Huntsville, AR. 1993.
The Legend of Starcrash,
Ozark Mountain Publishing, 1994.
The Legacy from the Stars,
Ozark Mountain Publishing, 1996.
The Custodians,
Ozark Mountain. Publishing, 1999.
www.dolorescannon.com

Carroll, Lee & Kryon
The End Times
The Kryon Writings Publishing, Del Mar, CA, 1993.
The Great Shift, Weiser Books, San Francisco, CA, 2009.
www.kryon.com

Carter, Rev. Michael J.S.
Alien Scriptures—Extraterrestrials in the Holy Bible
Grave Distractions Publications, Nashville, TN, 2013.
www.michaeljscarter.com

Cayce, Edgar
The Edgar Cayce Collection
General Editor Hugh Lynn Cayce
Bonanza Books, New York, NY, 1986.

Hopkins, Budd
Witnessed
Pocket Books, New York, NY, 1996.
Missing Time
Ballantine Books, New York, NY, 1981.
Intruders
Penguin Group,London, England, 1987.

Jacobs, David M. Ph.D.
Secret Life
Simon & Schuster, New York, NY, 1992.
www.ufoabduction.com

Jung, Carl G. and others
Man and His Symbols
Dell Publishing Co., Inc., New York, NY, 1964.

Mack, John E., M.D.
Abduction
Macmillan Publishing Co., New York, NY, 1994.

Moss, Robert,
Conscious Dreaming
Crown Trade Paperbacks, New York, NY, 1996.
www.mossdreams.com

Newton, Michael, Ph.D.
Journey of Souls
Llewellyn Publishing, St. Paul, MN, 2003.
http://michaelnewtonphd.com

Red Star, Nancy
Star Ancestors
Destiny Books, Rochester, VT, 2000.
www.nancyredstar.com

Romanek, Stan
Messages
Llewellyn Publications, Woodbury, MN, 2009.
Answers
Etherean, LLC, Colorado, 2011.
The Orion Regressions
Etherean, LLC, Colorado, 2011.
www.stanromanek.com

Romanek, Lisa
From My Side of the Bed
Etherean, LLC, Colorado, 2011.
www.lisaromanek.com

Sparks, Jim
The Keepers
Wild Flower Press, Columbus, NC, 2008.
http://jim-sparks.com

Strieber, Whitley
Confirmation
St. Martin's Press, New York, NY, 1998.
Transformation
Avon Books, New York, NY, 1989.
The Secret School, HarperCollins, New York, NY, 1997.
Breakthrough
HarperCollins, New York, NY, 1995.
The Key, Walker & Collier, Inc., New York, NY, 2011.
www.unknowncountry.com

Strieber, W. & Bell, Art
The Coming Global Superstorm
Pocket Books, New York, NY, 1999.

Targ, Russell
Limitless Mind
New World Library, Novato, CA, 2004.
www.espresearch.com

Tessman, Diane
The UFO Agenda
Eye Scry Publications, Yucca Valley, CA, 2013.
Earth Changes Bible
Inner Light Publications, New Brunswick, NJ, 1996.
www.earthchangepredictions.com

Walters, Ed & Frances
UFO Abductions in Gulf Breeze
Avon Books New York, NY, 1994.

Wilcock, David
The Source Field Investigations
Penguin Group, New York, NY, 2011.
The Synchronicity Key
Penguin Group, New York, NY, 2013.
www.DivineCosmos.com

Wilson, Katharina
The Alien Jigsaw
Puzzle Publishing, Portland, OR, 1995.

Other:

Hymn Title: *Lead, Kindly Light*
Lyricist/Poet: John H. Newman, 1833.
The Pilgrim Press Boston, MA, Chicago, IL.
©1931 by Sidney A. Weston; Revised Edition ©1935.

About the Dreamer

The physical body may age but the "essence of our being" is ageless.

Joan Bridgeman, the Dreamer, is pictured above. She is the younger, dark-haired personification of the self who appears in her dreams.

About the Author

Joan Bridgeman has enjoyed many artistic skills during her lifetime. She has been a music educator, an arranger and composer, a vocal performer, an actress and is now author of two books.

Born in New York and raised in Massachusetts, Joan lived and worked in four different New England states until 1979, when she moved to North Carolina and put down roots.

She has two sons, two grandsons and now lives happily in Southern Pines with her husband and their two cats.

Contact:

Karen Mireau
Publisher
AZALEA ART PRESS
Azalea.Art.Press@gmail.com
http://azaleaartpress.blogspot.com/

Joan Bridgeman
Author
Secret.Contact.Book@gmail.com
http://dreamguided.blogspot.com/